ALL TUCKED IN...

Jule McBride

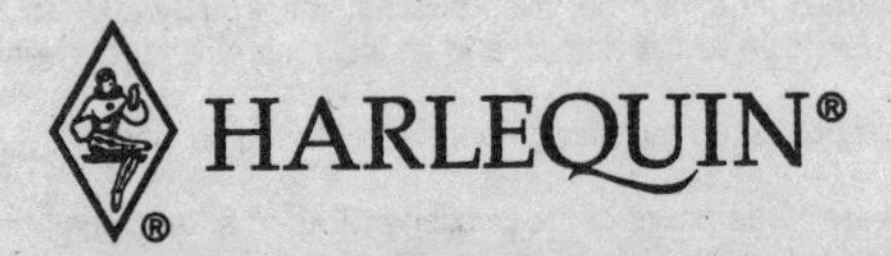

TORONTO • NEW YORK • LONDON
AMSTERDAM • PARIS • SYDNEY • HAMBURG
STOCKHOLM • ATHENS • TOKYO • MILAN • MADRID
PRAGUE • WARSAW • BUDAPEST • AUCKLAND

For Birgit,
for her saintly patience with this deadline,
and for so deserving all the good things that are coming her way!

ISBN 0-373-79095-3

ALL TUCKED IN...

This edition published by arrangement with Harlequin Books S.A.

Visit us at www.eHarlequin.com

Printed in U.S.A.

Blaze™

Dear Reader,

Like most people, I've always been fascinated by dreams, the unconscious and the elusive images that often haunt us for years, swirling in our minds like fairy dust looking for the right place to land.

All Tucked In… proved to be such a landing place. The sexy hero, Dr. Tobias Free, has become a dream researcher in order to cure his ex-fiancée of the nightmares that haunt her. But sparks really fly when his cure works better than expected, turning her nightmares into hot dreams about him!

I hope *All Tucked In…* will tuck you in and keep you up well into the night!

Very best,

Jule McBride

Books by Jule McBride

HARLEQUIN BLAZE

67—THE SEX FILES

HARLEQUIN TEMPTATION

875—THE HOTSHOT*
883—THE SEDUCER*
891—THE PROTECTOR*

*Big Apple Bachelors Trilogy

"Why don't you come back to bed?" Carla whispered

Tobias hesitated even as his gaze burned down every inch of her body. "*Back* to bed?"

Carla frowned. Had she heard right? Or was she confusing her dreams with reality again?

His voice was husky. "Uh...you sure?"

"After last night?" She smiled in invitation. "Absolutely."

He paused, then unbuttoned his shirt and let it shrug from powerful, sleek shoulders. His jeans were unsnapped next, the bulge of his masculinity unmistakable. "Climb in," she offered, her mind racing with the events of the past two nights. "Am I dreaming?"

Grinning, he reached over and gently pinched her cheek. "How's that feel?"

She pushed the sheet aside in welcome. Another look of indecision crossed his features. "You're overdressed," she complained, putting her arms around his neck. As images from their previous night's lovemaking flashed through her mind, she snuggled against his hard body. "And I was counting on a repeat performance...."

Judging by the arousal beneath the fly of his jeans, Tobias was more than ready to oblige her.

1

THIS WAS HARDLY THE FIRST time Dr. Tobias Free wished he hadn't discovered steel baron Cornelius Sloane's nineteenth-century pornography collection. In fact, the only other thing in life that had caused Tobias more sleepless nights was Carla DiDolche, the Italian spitfire who'd left him at the altar seven years ago. Now he surveyed the "artwork" spread across the boardroom table, his eyes trailing over a few pieces before settling on an ink drawing of a whip-wielding woman in a bustier and frilly pantaloons, a pencil sketch of three topless chorus girls, and a watercolor of a man in cross-tied breeches having his crotch fondled.

Then Tobias looked around the crowded board table.

"Well," Margaret Craig was saying to J. J. Sloane the seventh, sole heir to Cornelius Sloane's fortune, "we all know how much this ancestral mansion has meant to you, since you used to live here, Mr. Sloane, and we also know how much it means now—" She shot a piercing, significant look at Tobias "—to the University of Pittsburgh, which has been using it to house its sleep clinic research facility for the past ten years." Margaret paused for a deep breath. "However—and I'm speaking for every member of the Pittsburgh Preservation Society, not to mention the community at large—we feel it's our duty to open this mansion to the public, especially since Dr. Free has discovered such a vast vault of art...."

J. J. Sloane, whom Tobias secretly referred to as Sloane Junior, was a tall, thin, overly pretty, silver-haired playboy who'd just hit forty and begun to realize that he was an only child with no heirs. He leaned forward, looking interested. "Does the Society really think it could do something with the mansion? Something for posterity that we'd be remembered by?"

"Of course!" Margaret assured him, squaring her matronly shoulders. "We're prepared to make this your legacy, Mr. Sloane. Stone mansions of this magnitude are rarely found intact, as you can imagine! Most of the places along this part of Fifth Avenue, which we Pittsburghers so fondly refer to as mansion row, have been turned into apartments or businesses. And yet this remained a private home until you left in the nineties, sir, which makes it very special. Its architecture is gorgeous. The extensive grounds are divine. Even the astonishing stone fountain just off the veranda is in working order. With the exception of the Frick mansion in the Point Breeze neighborhood, few buildings in Pittsburgh are this impressive...."

Sloane leaned further forward. "You really think it compares to the Frick museum?"

"Absolutely!"

"And the Preservation Society would...?"

"The plans—and let me tell you, we have many, Mr. Sloane—are all included in the prospectus in front of you. We'd like to offer tours of the mansion, as well as lectures about the many contributions the Sloanes have made to our city. Maybe open a gift shop. Possibly even lend books from the extensive library. And of course, we'll be opening a gallery, not only for the photographs displayed in this room, but also for the new art found by Dr. Free...."

Tobias's eyes shifted to the pornographic pictures again, landing on a charcoal drawing of a woman removing veils as she danced. Most of the stuff wasn't that racy, at least not by comparison to today's Guess ads, but in the late 1800s, it must have been as hot as tamales.

Tobias shook his head. Under any other circumstances, he would have laughed. Yes, watching the members of the Preservation Society—mostly prim elderly ladies like Margaret with blue-rinsed hair and American flag pins proudly affixed to the lapels of their linen suits—sit around trying to elevate a porn collection to the level of high art would have brought a chuckle.

Except that Tobias's ten-year lease on this building was over in a month, and these sweet little ladies were truly going to snap his dream clinic out from under him. Having finally realized he lacked heirs, Sloane had become determined to do something to give his life meaning. As near as Tobias could tell, turning forty had been a rude awakening, and now Sloane hoped the Preservation Society could lend his previously dissipated life some credibility.

To add insult to injury, Tobias had once married Margaret Craig's daughter, Sandy—this was after Carla DiDolche, of course—and while the union had lasted only three disastrous months before it was annulled, Margaret had never forgiven him for leaving her daughter. Now she was relishing taking away the building in which Tobias housed his life's work. Oh, yeah, he thought now, eyeing her, Margaret definitely carried a grudge. Probably Sandy had told her mother the truth. That even after marrying another woman, Tobias simply couldn't get his mind off Carla.

Not that Tobias felt any guilt. He'd dated Sandy on the rebound and let her pressure him into marriage. When things hadn't worked out, she'd quickly remarried a mall developer from North Carolina who'd kept her in high style ever since. Last time she'd visited the Burgh for the holidays, she'd been pregnant with twins.

Shifting uncomfortably in his seat, Tobias tugged the knot at his throat, wishing he could take off his tie. He hated ties. In fact, the only thing more loathsome than ties were the jackets you had to wear with them. Unfortunately, even his best jeans and corduroy blazer couldn't hold a candle to the suits worn by his competitors. Last night, on the phone, his mother had urged him to go buy some dress slacks. Maybe he should have listened. She'd also mentioned Carla, the way she always did. After seven years, Laura Free still missed the young woman she'd been so sure was going to become her daughter-in-law. She and Sandy hadn't really hit it off.

Tobias blew out a sigh. What a couple of days! It didn't help that one of the three male members of the Pittsburgh Preservation Society was Vince Gato, owner of Gambolini and Gato Imports, which was a wine importing business on Liberty Avenue, at the opposite end of the block from DiDolche's, the family-owned café of which Carla was now the sole proprietor. From what Tobias recalled, the Gatos and DiDolches went way back. They'd known each other since the old country, which meant circa 1850.

Nope. Even after seven years, there was no escaping Carla. She intruded on his thoughts at the most unexpected times. Tobias suddenly realized that Sloane Junior was addressing him and even though Tobias hadn't actually seen Carla for awhile, he silently cursed her for breaking his concentration. "Yes, Mr. Sloane?"

"Once more," asked Sloane Junior, "how did you come across the drawings, Dr. Free?"

As if he didn't know. For some reason, Sloane Junior loved this story. Tobias retold the tale of how, a couple of months ago, when he and a colleague were moving some equipment, he'd inadvertently tripped, hit the side of a mantle in what had previously been Cornelius Sloane's study—only to have the wall swing inward, just like in an old horror movie, to expose a hidden room.

"What a find!" Margaret exclaimed breathlessly.

"Yes, indeed," seconded Vince Gato.

"And you were carrying one of those...what was it, Dr. Free?" asked Sloane Junior.

"An electroencephalograph," Tobias reminded him.

"Ah, yes. An electroencephalograph."

"Yes," Tobias added quickly, glad for the opportunity to speak his piece since, as far as he was concerned this meeting had definitely focused too much on the Preservation Society's concerns. "The electroencephalograph is an incredible piece of equipment. It allows researchers to chart brain activity during sleep by attaching electrodes to the head. And as you know, because of the long-term lease we negotiated in the past, we have been able to make great headway in our research."

Sloane Junior barely looked interested. "Hmm."

"It's really because of you, sir," Tobias forced himself to repeat, "that we've been able to make such great strides in sleep and dream research. And not just in better-known areas such as insomnia, narcolepsy or sleep apnea, but most importantly in the area of guided dream imagery."

As he spoke, Tobias's eyes settled on one of the old sepia-toned daguerreotype photographs that graced the walls, this one of turn-of-the-century construction on Liberty Avenue in the block that would eventually house both Gato and Gambolini's as well as Di-Dolche's café. Once more, he pushed away an image of Carla, and yet she always remained in his mind, running under his conscious thoughts like the unseen current in a river. Her image intruded when he least expected it, least wanted it, and, in this case, most resented it. Right now, he needed to concentrate. "We really feel, if given the chance, that the research we do here will change people's lives."

"Yes, yes," said Sloane Junior. "I read the article in *Newsweek.*"

He sounded so dismissive. Was this dissipated playboy really going to turn a research facility into an art gallery for hundred-year-old porn? As soon as Tobias had stumbled upon the art, the Preservation Society had started angling to open the mansion to the public. "Already—" Tobias forced himself to smile as he continued "—we've helped countless people who suffer from nocturnal eating syndrome and REM behavioral disorder." He implored Sloane Junior with his eyes. Couldn't the other man see how important this work was? "We've done exemplary work with troubled children plagued by nightmares," he explained. "And now, we're really making exciting headway with guided dreams, which promises all sorts of therapeutic uses..."

As he spoke, his voice quickened with passion. If he hadn't been so attached to his work, he'd never have survived the humiliation, not to mention emotional pain, of Carla's bolting back down the aisle. After that, discounting his brief marriage to Sandy, he'd worked at this clinic around the clock. "We've made progress translating electrical impulses into written accounts of what people dream about," he said. "In other words, we're identifying patterns that will allow us to examine your brain waves and tell you what you're dreaming. Someday our researchers will even be able to watch your dreams on a screen...."

One of the Preservationists gave in and voiced curiosity. "You mean, you'll be able to watch someone's dreams, like a movie?"

"We hope," Tobias said just as another lady elbowed the first for showing interest.

Sloane Junior lifted his chin. "Do you really believe you'll be able to do that?"

Tobias nodded. "Already, by monitoring brain waves, we can make a fair guess as to what you're dreaming. During guided dream experiments, we've discovered we can deliver electronic impulses to disturbed sleepers and change the content of their dreams.

We've been able to change nightmares into pleasant dreams. As you know—''

Sloane Junior raised a staying hand. ''We'll get back to that, Dr. Free. And thank you for the input. For now, however, I'm ready to announce that I'll be spending the next two weeks at the clinic while I make my decision. I know that you've—'' he nodded at Tobias ''—accomplished a lot here. And yet, because this mansion is part of my heritage, it may be best to turn it over to the Preservation Society.

''Within two weeks, I should be able to decide the future of the mansion. Meantime...'' He chuckled. ''I don't know about the group, but I'm starved, and judging by my watch, it's lunchtime.''

Smiling around the table, he added, ''Dr. Free has arranged for us to dine in the day room. Shall we?''

Everyone nodded assent.

Tobias tried not to let his temper get the best of him. He'd hardly wanted to feed the very people who were about to dismantle his dream clinic, but he didn't want to appear ungracious. Years ago, he'd needed a science lab, not this drafty mansion, but when he'd landed a grant and found this place, he'd made do, turning it into one of the country's most prestigious clinics. As much as he'd hoped the University would set him up in a space better suited to his work, competition for funding was fierce. Between the University of Pittsburgh, Carnegie-Melon and Dusquene University, Tobias Free was hardly the only academic in town who needed to house a research facility. If he lost the lease, he—not to mention all the people who'd worked for him for the past ten years—might be out of a job.

As he stood and lifted a briefcase, his eyes strayed to the old photographs on the wall. Taken when Pittsburgh was a boomtown, they were all yellow-toned, depicting crowded streets and skies made dark by smoke pouring from Cornelius Sloane's steel mills. Some showed barges marked with the Sloane name that had once traveled choked rivers, transporting steel. Others showed the tenements Cornelius Sloane had built to house the immigrants who'd worked for him, many of whom had been Italian.

Tobias's eyes settled on Carla's block in Bloomfield, and he visualized the Italian neighborhood as it was today, complete with the West Penn Hospital, the Paddy Cake Bakery and Tessaro's restaurant. Unfortunately, his mind zeroed in on the Church of the Immaculate Conception—and everything else came in a flash: the white aisle runner, the crowded pews, his four buddies leading her four girlfriends down an aisle strewn with red and white rose petals.

For a second, Tobias's heart welled with the love he'd felt when he'd seen Carla in the strapless wedding dress. Wild black curly hair had spilled like corkscrewed ribbons over her bare shoulders, and white satin showed off a gorgeous figure made full by the endless Italian feasts her mama served. From under the veil had been only hints of her face, the dark eyes and wine-red lips that Tobias still dreamed about. She'd been only five steps away, almost in his arms, when she'd suddenly gasped, turned on the heel of a slender, white-beaded slipper, and run back down the aisle.

Pulling himself back to reality, Tobias began leading toward the day room, only to have one of the elderly women—he wasn't sure, but he thought her name was Agnes—politely curl a hand around his upper arm and ask, "What made you decide to work in the field of dreams, anyway, Dr. Free?"

For the same reason he'd done many things in his life: Carla. Tobias managed a shrug as he guided the woman through the doorway. "Oh. I don't know. I started out in biochemical research. One thing led to another."

It was only the partial truth. Really, he'd wanted to cure Carla's insomnia. She was so hot, so passionate, so full of life. But she sometimes couldn't sleep through a night. After their lovemaking, he'd witnessed the torture she endured in her sleep. Not only were her dreams so real that she'd become convinced they'd happened, but she'd also had a bizarre recurring dream about golden underwear.

Over and over, from as far back as Carla could remember, she'd dreamed of seeing a man seated at a shadowy desk in a dark, dank room she couldn't identify. Each time, the dream was the same. The man would slowly lift a pair of sparkling underwear made of gold.

It might have been funny, except that Carla would awaken feeling terrorized. He'd held her, too. Even now, he could remember the heat of her soft, well-loved body. She was nothing like Sandy Craig, the woman he'd married. While Sandy was angles and points, Carla was curves and cushions. So feminine, too. With her trembling in his arms, not wanting to let go, he'd never felt like more of a man. Everything about her had made him feel...strong. Protective. Necessary.

Briefly shutting his eyes as he guided the woman toward the day room, Tobias envisioned Carla's repeating dream, conjuring the dark dank room, the man lifting the gold underwear. And then, very close to Carla's ear, the man's voice would sound, saying, "If you marry, you will die."

As far as Tobias knew, that was the real reason Carla DiDolche had run from the altar on their wedding day.

THE BELT!

His palms broke out in a sweat as his eyes drifted nervously over the drawings left on the table. The picture of the belt was nearly buried under the others. His fingers itched to touch it. Somehow, he had to get it.

"Aren't you going to the day room with the others?" asked Margaret Craig.

Surveying her buxom, matronly form, the blue-rinsed hair and bright blue eyes, he forced a smile. "Just enjoying the art," he said, shaking his head, glad to hear that his voice sounded steady. "It's such an incredible find."

"If we get the lease," Margaret agreed, "these pictures, not to mention the mansion itself, will be available to the public." She smiled. "And then I'll feel I've done my duty to the community."

Shoving his hands into his pockets, he watched her begin gently lifting the pictures from the table. Arranging them between pieces of parchment paper, she placed them into a portfolio.

He swallowed hard, hating how tight his chest felt. All the air seemed to have been sucked from the room. He could scarcely breathe. "Are the pictures catalogued?'' he managed, hoping he sounded only casually curious.

She frowned. ''You know, it's funny you ask. I believe so, though, now that you mention it, I don't know who took care of the matter. It would have been someone in the Society.''

Was it possible she was wrong?

Warding off an excited shudder, he eyed the picture he wanted...the picture he had to have. Of course, the picture of the golden chastity belt was nothing compared to the genuine article, a priceless relic that belonged to him.

Yes, it was his. His alone. Believed to date from the earliest of the Crusades, the gold chastity belt carried a power all its own. The glint of its metal reflected the darker times when it was forged, and bespoke unholy alliances, sieges and slaughters. Those wars and skirmishes were rivaled only by the jealousy of the men who left their women behind, and who'd ensured by any means necessary that they'd never be touched by another man....

The belt was beautiful, the name of its owner lost to time and history. His heart hammered. Sweat beaded on his lip. He'd loved to have seen a woman wear it, he thought, imagining someone young and dark-haired. He could see how the heavy gold would tightly encircle her waist, locking in back.

Only when he heard a chuckle did he remember Margaret Craig was still beside him. Realizing he'd been staring at the picture of the belt, he quickly glanced away, cursing himself. He needed to steal the picture, but he couldn't even contain his interest, so that Margaret wouldn't notice.

"Quite something, isn't it?" she said. "Golden underwear." Offering a schoolgirl's giggle, she lifted the watercolor.

Only from the back, he thought. Once turned around, the chastity belt was encrusted with priceless jewels...diamonds, rubies and emeralds that made him salivate every time he saw them.

"Someone had a naughty imagination," said Margaret.

Only he knew the chastity belt was real, not just the subject of an artist's picture. He worked to tamp down the sudden dark anger that churned within him. He had to get the picture Margaret Craig was putting into the portfolio! Before today, he'd never even known this picture existed. Years ago, Cornelius Sloane must have seen the picture first, then tracked down the genuine article, to add to his collection....

Realizing Margaret was speaking to him, he lifted his gaze.

"Ready for lunch?"

His throat tightened. "Would you like me to put the pictures away for you?" Could he somehow steal the picture now, without getting caught?

"They go in the safe downstairs. I'll take care of it."

The safe downstairs? Could he get the combination? How had he managed not to see this picture before today? He'd joined the Preservation Society hoping to find information about the belt, especially any documents that might identify the original owners. But now...the picture had to be destroyed. If it was made public, hung in a gallery in the Sloane mansion, there was a possibility Carla DiDolche might see it someday.

And Carla, who had dreamed of golden underwear, might realize the truth: that what she'd dreamed wasn't really a figment of her imagination, but a dangerous reality....

"MA, YOU AND POP CAN'T visit," Carla DiDolche muttered into the portable phone as she took a final glance around the apartment, wondering if she was forgetting anything. She'd shared this place with her parents years ago, before she'd moved to Oakland where she'd intended to live with Tobias after they married. Two years ago, after her parents retired to Florida, Carla had moved back home. Since she was running the café downstairs now, it was more convenient. "I love you dearly," she continued. "But if you and Pop visit, you'll criticize everything I've done to the café."

Her mother gasped in horror. "We would never do that!"

"Oh, yes, you would," returned Carla, heading downstairs. As she opened the lower door and headed into the café, she was relieved to see Jenna already hard at work, standing behind one of the espresso makers.

Despite how tired she felt this morning, Carla smiled and took a deep breath, filling her lungs with the scents of her childhood. A hundred percent pure Italian coffee, she thought. There was, quite simply, nothing like it. Almost every morning of her life, she'd breathed the heady scent that had always been the DiDolches' lifeblood. Waving at Vince Gato, who was seated near the front windows with Sylvia Rossetti and Salvatore Domico, Carla beelined for Jenna, saying, ''Is mine ready?''

''Coming right up, boss,'' returned the other woman cheerfully. A moment later, Jenna turned. She was dressed in black, and when she grinned, the silver loop in her eyebrow flashed every bit as much as the smile. She set a heavy white cup and saucer on the counter. ''This is that new Kenyan blend you wanted to try.''

''Kenya?'' Mary DiDolche said into the phone. ''Did I hear Jenna say Kenyan blend? You know we've never used that. Your father gets his shipments from Jack Liotta in the Strip District.''

''Mama,'' Carla cut in, gripping the phone more tightly and trying her best not to lose her temper as she lifted the glass lids of the cake plates on the counter and carefully scrutinized cookies and pastries. In about fifteen minutes, the morning rush was going to begin. ''I know how you and Pop feel about expanding our repertoire, but Starbucks is killing us. Besides, the Kenyan beans did come from Mr. Liotta.''

Her mother made a shocked sound. ''Jack Liotta has quit selling Italian products?''

''Of course not. But he knows that we have to expand our menu. Just as he has to expand his. To keep up with the times.''

''We have our faithful customers,'' her mother said defensively.

''I know, Ma, but...'' Sighing, Carla decided not to point out that her parents' friends weren't going to be around forever. ''We need to bring in new customers. The Marcottis retired to Florida around the time you did. And the Tuccis are trying to sell their place.''

"Vince Gato is still loyal to us," claimed her mother.

"True," Carla said, shooting Vince a quick grin. "He's having his espresso right now, but we need more than one customer, now, don't we?" Actually, there were seven in the shop. Not bad for this time of the morning, but if her parents would let her offer breakfast cereals, she could pull in some of the college kids. Lifting the lid of a cake dish, she took one of the decadent, sugar-loaded morning pastries that DiDolche's had been serving the public, along with its turbo coffee, since 1888. "I take it Louie got here," she said to Jenna as she took a bite, tucking the phone beneath her chin, "but where's the tiramisu?"

On the phone, her mother inhaled audibly. "Did you just say there's no tiramisu?"

"Calm down, Ma," Carla said as she chewed. "If Louie didn't bring all the cakes, he'll be back, okay?"

"He'd better."

Carla laughed softly. "If he doesn't, I'll call cousin Carmine, okay?" Carmine, who owned a locksmith business, was generally acknowledged as the toughest of all the DiDolche relatives.

"Carmine knows how to handle things," agreed her mother.

Carla was still busy doing her usual morning once-over. The plate glass windows were gleaming, and she felt a surge of pride as she took in the green, gold-tipped lettering on the glass that read DiDolche's Since 1888.

It was a wonderful café. Above, was the original tin ceiling; below, black-and-white marble floor tiles deeply veined with green. Curved-glass cases were chock-full of the rich, homemade Italian deserts Louie delivered every morning, and fresh daisies in vases graced marble-topped tables on iron stands laden with scrollwork. Carla frowned as her eyes settled on the green bench outside. ''Mrs. Domico's poodle is by our bench again,'' Carla reported.

''That woman!'' exclaimed her mother, outraged. ''She never picks up after that awful animal.''

Through the plate glass, Carla caught Mrs. Domico's eye and mouthed the words, Pick up. To her mother, she said, ''Don't worry. I just told her.''

''Good!'' said her mother. Before Carla could start arguing once more about the changes she needed to make to keep their business in the black, her mother continued, ''It's nearly eight. Why are you just now getting downstairs? It's those dreams again, isn't it, Carla? You didn't sleep last night, did you?''

''I'm fine,'' promised Carla.

''No, you're not. And if you can't sleep, you can't run a business. DiDolche's has been around since 1888.''

The words put the fear of God into Carla. ''I can run a business just fine.'' At moments like this, it was hard to believe her parents had retired and lived in another state. If they decided to reclaim the business, Carla would be crushed. As far back as she could remember, she'd wanted to run this place. ''I have a business degree, Ma. And you're not coming here to go over the books.'' If her father saw that she'd introduced three new kinds of coffee, she'd be in deep moose caca.

''I knew it when I called and you were still upstairs

in the apartment,'' said her mother, ignoring her. ''It's those dreams.''

''I'm fine,'' Carla assured her just as her eyes landed on the *Pittsburgh Post Gazette.* The headline read Pittsburgh Preservation Society May Take Over Sloane Mansion. Her heart lurching, she edged closer and began reading. What on earth had happened? Was Tobias going to lose his clinic? That place was his life! Her cheeks warmed as she thought of how happy he'd been when he'd gotten the lease ten years ago—they'd had dinner at Tessaro's to celebrate—then she mentally flashed on their wedding and how she'd run back down the aisle.

And then Carla firmly reminded herself that Tobias had married Sandy Craig, who was definitely everything Carla wasn't: tall, thin, blond and Protestant.

She forced herself to finish reading the article. Of course, through Vince Gato who was a member of the Preservation Society, she'd known that Tobias had discovered Cornelius Sloane's hidden porn collection, but she'd not known that he could lose his lease. Wouldn't the university give him more funding, for another space he could turn into a clinic?

If not, what would he do? A dream researcher of his caliber would probably have to relocate to work. He'd even been written up in *Newsweek.* Somehow, she simply couldn't stand the idea of him leaving the Burgh. This was his home. Even though they barely spoke anymore, she and Tobias had begun dating in high school, and he was the only man she'd ever slept with. Even though they weren't in love, he was...

Hers.

It didn't matter that she'd caught him trying to avoid

her when they'd bumped into each other in a grocery store last month. Deep down, she knew that if she ever really needed something, she could call on him.

"Are you listening, Carla?" demanded her mother.

"I was reading an article about Tobias," she admitted.

"See!" her mother exclaimed as if she'd just won a long-standing argument. "You still think about him! You can't get over him! He never leaves your mind!"

"He's in the paper, Ma," she said defensively. "It sounds like the clinic might close."

Her mother offered another of her trademark, theatrical gasps. "Well, this means you'd better make an appointment and see if he can cure you, Carla."

"Ma," she managed as two customers came in, signaling the beginning of the rush hour, "I've really got to go. I need to look at the air conditioner." It had gone on the blink for an hour yesterday. Not good, in the middle of August. Carla glanced longingly at a strip of unused ground beside the building. It would be the perfect place to build a patio and serve drinks—if only her parents would allow her to make the change.

Carla suddenly looked at Jenna and squinted. "Why are you here? Didn't you have a doctor's appointment?"

Jenna's eyes widened. "Uh...nope."

Her mother heaved a sigh. "It's those dreams again."

And it was, as much as Carla didn't want to admit it. Months had passed in nocturnal bliss, but then suddenly, last night, Carla had tossed and turned. She'd awakened with damp sheets twisted around her body.

Right now, she could absolutely swear she and Jenna had had a conversation about her taking the day off.

Yes. The memory was razor-sharp, as clear as this hot, scorching day promised to be. Jenna was standing near the counter, wearing a black sundress.

And yet it was only a dream.

The nightmare had returned, too. Carla could recall hazy visions of mazes and secret passageways. Stairs that led to nowhere. A dark, enclosed, musty-smelling cramped room where a man seated at a desk slowly lifted a pair of golden underwear. Golden underwear! What a crazy notion! So crazy that the dream shouldn't have been scary, and yet it was. Carla had never been able to make sense of it. Now she shuddered. Because, for a second, she could almost hear his voice at her ear, saying, "If you marry, you will die."

"Carla?" her mother was saying. "Carla?"

She snapped back to attention. "Huh?"

"This settles it," she said. "Your father and I are coming to Pittsburgh next week. No ifs, ands or buts. I want to know what you're doing at the café. The DiDolches have had this business—"

"Since 1888. I know, Ma. If you and Pop would start having some faith in me—"

Once more, her mother gasped. "We have faith in you!" she defended quickly. "You're our daughter! You're a DiDolche! We love you!"

Despite how drained she felt from the lack of sleep, Carla finally smiled. "I know you do."

"So, we're coming next week. And while we're there, you're going to take a few days off and go to that dream clinic, huh? What do you say, Carla?"

She slid her eyes to the newspaper article again, and her heart did that awful telltale flip-flop. Oh, she'd never forgive him for marrying Sandy Craig, but she guessed when it came to hurting each other, they were now even. And yes, he'd definitely hurt her. Deeply. Not that it made any more sense than her dreams, since it was she—not he—who had run out on the wedding. Still…just thinking about seeing him made her whole system start going off kilter. His name alone could give her sweating palms, a racing pulse, a melting core. You name it.

"Carla," her mother was saying, "as soon as we hang up this phone, you get right back on it, call the clinic and get yourself an appointment."

Carla hedged. "Ma…"

"If you don't, your father and I might have to come back home and help with the café…."

Carla's lips parted. "You know you're matchmaking, don't you?" Before her mother could answer, she added, "It really is over between me and Tobias, Mama." Their near-marriage was seven years ago, past history. She still wasn't completely sure why she'd run. Was it really because of some stupid dream? Was she that haunted by phantoms of her own imagination? By things that weren't even real?

"I'm not matchmaking!" her mother was saying. "I'm worried about your health. And if you don't make an appointment with Tobias, I'm afraid you'll be too tired to run the café. The DiDolches have been in business—"

"Since 1888. I know, Ma." If she'd heard it once, she'd heard it a thousand times. Lifting her mug from the counter, Carla decided to ignore her mother's veiled threats about reclaiming the café; she took a deep draught of coffee. The new Kenyan blend was going to be a keeper, she realized instantly. "You know what happened at the church, Ma," she finally said. "I can't make an appointment with Tobias."

"You can't," her mother rejoined decisively. "But you will." Another audible breath sounded. "Or else I really will come back and run the café myself."

"You're not serious," Carla muttered. But then, when it came to the manipulations of Mary DiDolche, one never knew. Carla hesitated, then she thought of last night, which had been pure hell. Then she had an image of her parents coming back to town and working in the café again. "Okay," she agreed. "I'll call the clinic. I promise."

"If any man can turn a woman's nightmares into dreams," declared her mother on a relieved sigh, "it's probably Tobias Free."

And how, thought Carla. Mothers might know best, but they usually didn't know the half of it.

2

"CARLA," TOBIAS SAID, extending his hand. "I saw your name on the roster. This is a surprise."

An unpleasant one? It was hard to tell by his tone. "Hello, Tobias." As she said his name, Carla's heart missed a beat. Just eyeing the big strong hand that, in the past, had slowly, dexterously caressed every inch of her sent prickles dancing across her skin. When she slid her palm to his, her breath stilled completely. The handshake was quick, firm and businesslike, and yet not quick enough, since Carla instantly registered the smooth feel of his fingers. Her belly fluttered as they ghosted over hers. The muscles of her lower body tightened as they withdrew. Tingles made the tips of her breasts constrict, and she could only hope he hadn't noticed.

Yeah, she reflected, that hand was just as she remembered: warm, dry to the touch and intriguingly alive. She tried not to take the thoughts any further…to how that hand had felt sliding up the creamy skin of her shuddering inner thighs. He could caress her for hours, bringing her to satisfaction over and over. He was the kind of man who loved every second of a woman's pleasure….

Heat suffused her cheeks. The room was air-conditioned, but suddenly every interior inch of her felt as if it had hit triple-digit temperatures in August. Maybe even the depths of Hades. Right about now, she'd kill for an ice cube. A bead of sweat snaked between her breasts and she exhaled shakily. No, she never should have let her mother bully her into coming here.

"Have a seat," he suggested in a voice that could have been whispering sweet naughty nothings into her ears for the past seven years.

Vaguely, she realized she was staring at his mouth as if mesmerized. What had she been thinking? Lord, Carla, she thought now. You could have married this luscious hunk.

No, Carla hadn't forgotten the voice any more than the feel of his hands. Deep and rich, it had seemed to rumble in his chest like thunder before a storm, then pour out like sweet, succulent honey. "Seat?" she echoed, her mind ceasing to function as her eyes dropped over his body—the wide, broad shoulders, the hard chest, the jeans that were just tight enough to gracefully trace his masculinity. But why was Tobias wearing a sport coat and tie? If he was still the man Carla had known, his employers were lucky to get him to wear a shirt. Or anything at all. Yes...the Tobias Free she'd known had been very anti-clothes.

His lips were curling into the slow, sexy smile she remembered—and with that smile, the whole of their history threatened to overwhelm her. "Seat," he said, chuckling and pointing to a velvet upholstered love seat. "That thing you put your rear end on."

Hmm. So he still had a sense of humor. "Just wanted to make sure," she quipped. "I'd hate to wind up being a centerpiece for your table."

"Or hanging from a chandelier."

"You have that much fun around here, huh?"

"You'd be amazed where sleepwalkers wind up."

"Not really," she returned, thinking of her own nocturnal habits. Relaxing a little as she sat, she glanced around the fancy, old-fashioned parlor, taking in the red carpet and dark wood-paneled walls. "The place hasn't changed a bit," she added, then wished she hadn't said the words since they were another reminder that she'd been here with him before.

"Yeah," he agreed simply, taking a clipboard from under his arm as he turned away to seat himself on a settee opposite her. "It's right out of a Stephen King novel. If you ask me, this mansion looks haunted."

"Good for a dream clinic," she offered.

"Only if you're having nightmares."

"Which I still am."

"I can see that from your intake form."

She could barely believe they were talking like two normal, rational people. No doubt it wouldn't last long. Their only real conversation after she'd run from the altar had quickly degenerated into a screaming match. She wasn't interested in having a replay. Neither was he. Ever since, on the rare occasions they'd spoken, the conversations had been brief and polite. They were adults, after all.

As he scanned down the form she'd filled out when she'd arrived, she took another look around the room, mulling over the details—a mosaic fireplace, crown ceiling moldings and ancient oil paintings. Original beaded lamps from the nineteenth century were perched on end tables, and the hammered bronze candelabra on the mantle looked like something Dracula might carry up a flight of stairs. Tobias was right. The mansion, which had been leased with most of its original furnishings, did look a little spooky, like something out of a horror story. "It's not really scary," she decided aloud.

"No," he agreed. "Just old."

She shifted her gaze to Tobias, sucking in a breath when pure lust blindsided her again. Past memories of their lovemaking came, as visceral and unwanted as the dreams that so often seemed real to her. She found herself recalling the strength in his legs as they'd glided along her thighs, and how the short silken strands of his chest hair could feel, teasing the sensitive skin between her fingers.

He'd changed in the past seven years. Oh, he was still the same heartthrob who'd stolen her attention in high school, when he was a track star and she was a member of the pep club. He had the same straight, hay-blond hair that he wore too long and that occasionally dipped into melting brown eyes. The same sexy light-brown dot of a mole beside lips that could kiss like the devil. The same burning, penetrating concentration that he brought to every task, including lovemaking. But a few lines had appeared around his eyes, and the skin over his high cheekbones seemed more taut, making him look more mature. Yes, any trace of the boy had definitely left Tobias Free. He'd grown up completely, into a man.

He glanced up from the intake form. "Is this everything?"

Suddenly, she wished he wasn't being quite so businesslike, and that she was outfitted in something other than khaki pants and a T-shirt. Recently, she'd bought an emerald-green sundress, but she'd decided against wearing it, not wanting Tobias to think she'd dressed for him, if she saw him. It hadn't occurred to her that he'd sit down and read her intake form. She fought the urge to reach and smooth her hair, the wild curly strands of which were frizzing in the heat. "Yes," she said. "I really can't think of anything else."

"Before I show you to your room, I'd like to ask a couple more questions, if you don't mind."

He was showing her to her room? "Are you sure?" she managed, feeling more nervous by the minute. When she'd made the appointment, she'd convinced herself that she might not even see Tobias. "I mean..." She didn't know quite how to say it. "I didn't expect you to be involved in the..."

"Nitty-gritty? You know me better than that."

"So, that's how you think of me?" she couldn't help but tease. "As the nitty-gritty?"

His eyes captured hers. "Hands-on, if you prefer."

Heat slid through her veins again. He'd been hands-on in more ways than one. "I know how involved you are in your work," she answered, wondering if he'd actually just flirted with her. It was impossible to tell from his tone. "I'll be glad to answer anything I can, of course," she quickly added.

"How often do you suffer insomnia?"

She shrugged. "Not often anymore."

"Then why are you here?"

She'd forgotten that, too. He'd always gotten straight to the point. He was the same way in bed. He'd go straight for erogenous zones that sent her soaring. Suddenly, she wished she'd slept with some other man, if only once. That way, Tobias might not have such a hold over her fantasy life. "The dreams, when I do have them," she forced herself to say, "seem more—" she searched for a word "—intense."

"Intense?"

Like your melting brown eyes. "Yes."

"And they still seem real?"

She thought of the other morning, when she'd been so sure that Jenna had planned to take the day off work. "Very. Sometimes, I find myself assuming things happened that really didn't. For instance..." Furrowing her dark brows, she thought a moment. "The other day, when I saw Mrs. Domico walking her poodle, I was shocked because I'd thought Missy—that's her name—had been dyed green."

He laughed softly, and the sound warmed her blood. "Dyed green?"

She couldn't help but smile as she nodded. "I know it sounds crazy. Who would dye a dog green, but—"

"Mrs. Domico," Tobias interjected, thrusting the splayed fingers of a hand through his hair to get it out of his eyes. "From what I remember, she was just the type."

Carla laughed appreciatively, but the sound died abruptly on her lips. Tobias remembered everything, even Mrs. Domico. Was he as plagued by memories of their passion? "Well, the dog hadn't really been dyed green, of course. But as I passed Mrs. Domico on the street, I asked why she'd dyed Missy white again, instead of some other color. I said I thought she'd told me she was thinking about dying the dog blue, but..."

He quirked an eyebrow. "You actually had this conversation with Mrs. Domico?"

"Fortunately, people in the neighborhood are used to this quirk of mine," she reminded him. As her eyes drifted over Tobias, she couldn't help but suddenly frown.

He frowned back. "What?"

"Nothing," she said, then changed her mind and shrugged, eyeing his clothes, "I guess I'm just shocked by how respectable you've gotten."

"Sounds like resistance."

"Resistance?"

"Yeah." His lips turned upward, looking kissable. "Freud's concept. As soon as we start to analyze your dreams, he predicted you'd shift the subject."

She definitely wouldn't want Tobias to analyze the dreams she could so easily have about him. His gaze caught hers, locked and held. "About the outfit," he added. "Don't let a sport coat and tie fool you, Carla."

It wasn't really fooling her so much as making her salivate. "I don't think I've ever seen you in one."

It was the wrong thing to say. She could have kicked herself instantly. All at once, the air felt bristly, as if someone had come along with a syringe and injected it with pure, one-hundred-percent porcupine needles. Because, of course, he had worn a tie before. A tux, too. On their wedding day. To make up for the faux pas, she said, "It looks good."

Clearly fighting not to roll his eyes, he stared back down at the paper on the clipboard and resumed his businesslike tone. "Are the dreams the same?"

She nodded. "Yep. Ma insisted I try to get some help. I haven't had the...uh, underwear dream for awhile, but it's bothered me for the past few nights in a row."

"Your mother told you to come?"

Was it her imagination? Or, for the briefest instant, had he looked disappointed? Had he hoped this was an excuse to see him again? She hesitated. "Yes."

"How is your mom?"

"Fine." For a moment, she caught him up on her family, then asked about his, especially his mother, Laura, whom she missed. As he began reading her form again, she said, "According to the paper, you might lose the clinic. Is that really true?"

Looking vaguely annoyed, he lifted his chin once more, and somehow, she was glad to see the expression of his eyes soften when he registered her genuine concern. "Yeah," he said after a moment. He glanced over his shoulder toward a long entry hall. "Actually, that's the reason for the tie," he confessed. Before explaining, he continued. "I'm still so clueless when it comes to wearing them that Elsie had to knot the thing."

An image of Sandy Craig crowded into her mind. "Elsie?" she couldn't help but ask, trying to sound casual. Who was Elsie?

"Oh." His eyes widened slightly in surprise as if he'd expected her to know. "Elsie's my assistant."

She hoped she hadn't sounded jealous. Obviously, she had no right to the feeling. Her lips parted. "Cassandra's gone?"

He nodded. "Married a prof from Carnegie-Melon. What about Jenna?"

"She's still at the café. She got married, too."

"That mountain bike buff?"

She shook her head. "No. The tattoo artist."

Weddings were the last thing either one of them probably wanted to talk about, but Carla plunged on. "He has his own parlor now. The bike buff went to Alaska for a summer and never came back."

Another uncomfortable pause followed during which they tried to ignore the depth of their shared past and all the nuptial bliss that hadn't been theirs. In the silence, Carla actually felt her pulse quicken at the fantasy that he was lying, and that he'd actually dressed up for her, a notion he squelched by saying, "J. J. Sloane's in town. He's staying in the mansion, so you'll probably see him. He's trying to decide whether to give the next lease to me or to the Preservation Society."

"Ah. So, you're on best behavior."

He offered a droll expression she'd always loved that made him look uncharacteristically petulant and boyish. "Unfortunately."

You do so hate to be good. The words were on the tip of her tongue, and suddenly, she wanted to suggest that they be naughty…together. "The dreams are the same," she ventured instead, determined to get the interview back on track.

"Still having that golden underwear dream, huh?"

For a second, despite how the dream had often terrified her, she almost laughed. In the cold light of day, it seemed so ridiculous. She nodded. "Yes." Though talking about underwear with Tobias was right up there with the subject of marriage.

His brows furrowed in thought. Thick and bushy, they almost came together, forming a ledge. "And the sleepwalking?"

She shrugged. "That's hard to say. I live alone." Once more, there was the reminder that they'd planned to share a home, and she mentally flashed on the two-bedroom apartment further down Fifth Avenue, near the university, which they'd rented. She'd wound up living in it for three years. When he'd married Sandy Craig, she'd decided she needed a change, and after that move, of course, she'd ended up back in the apartment she'd previously shared with her parents.

"So you don't know if you sleepwalk?"

She shook her head.

"You don't wake up in places other than your own bed?"

"Uh...no, Tobias."

He sent her a long look. "I didn't mean it that way."

Good Catholic girl that she was, she figured Tobias knew she hadn't slept with anyone besides him. But maybe he'd actually been fishing. "Of course you didn't."

Once more, heat surged between them. A relationship was impossible, of course, she found herself thinking. After all, she'd left him at the altar, and then he'd married Sandy Craig. But Tobias was the only man she'd ever slept with—the only one she'd ever wanted to sleep with—and she'd definitely missed having sex. A lot. The truth was, Carla hadn't done it in seven years now. The way she'd been brought up, a woman only slept with her husband. Or at least the man she'd thought was going to be her husband.

Sucking in a breath, she collected her thoughts. "Sometimes, come to think of it, I do wake up on the couch,'' she said. ''As you know, Ma said I definitely sleepwalked as a kid.''

He jotted something in the margin of her intake sheet. ''Has anything changed in the dreams?''

''Changed?''

Chewing his lower lip, he thought a moment, shaking his head. ''I don't know. Is anything different?'' Shrugging, he added, ''Maybe about the room where the dream takes place? Does the man ever say anything new?''

As much as she hated visualizing the dream that had so often disturbed her, she shook her head. ''No. Everything's the same.''

He looked disappointed. ''Are you sure?''

She hated to say it. ''Absolutely.''

He sighed. ''Well...what I'd like to try tonight, assuming you have the nightmare, is some guided dream imagery.''

Now they were getting down to business, and she felt a rush of nervousness. Her hand tightened on the strap of the overnight duffel bag she'd nestled near her feet. ''Meaning?''

''When your nightmare's in progress, I'll administer electrical impulses.'' Interrupting himself as he stood, he added, ''It doesn't hurt. With any luck, it'll change the course of your nightmare.''

She stood also, feeling surprised when he took her bag. Why, she didn't know. Tobias was always a gentleman. Still, the bag wasn't heavy at all, so the gesture was unnecessary. She was squinting at him. ''Meaning?''

He considered. ''Well...various things can happen,'' he explained. ''I'll attach electrodes to your head, then when your nightmare begins, I'll send small jolts of electricity to your nerve endings.''

''Uh-huh,'' she murmured. Already, he was doing a fairly good job of that, so she could hardly wait for tonight.

''Patients say that something new happens in their dreams,'' he continued. ''For instance, the dark room in which it occurs might suddenly change into an enchanted forest, and the bad people are dealt with, maybe sent away by trusted friends. Or you might confront the man. Either way, the content of the dream changes just enough that you find your way out of it. It turns into a good story with a happy ending.''

She paused, fighting a shudder. She didn't want her repeating nightmare to occur tonight, much less to confront the man who'd haunted her for so many years. ''Great,'' she muttered. She was rewarded by the feel of Tobias's hand. It landed on the small of her back, and he used it to guide her through the doorway.

''Don't worry,'' he said, reassuringly. The creamy brown eyes that cut toward her settled on her face and didn't pull away. ''I'll be there all night, Carla.''

''You?'' Recollections of how he'd held her after her nightmares came back then, and she almost could feel his strong arms wrapping around her waist, pulling her close against his hard, naked body. All at once, she felt a rush of safety, just from the memory. But she also wondered what he was talking about. ''You'll be with me?''

He nodded. ''While you're sleeping, I'll be right on the other side of a glass partition. As soon as we get upstairs, you'll see.''

"A GLASS PARTITION," she murmured.

Tobias could tell she wasn't entirely happy with the setup. Not that he blamed her. He was just as uncomfortable. Was he really going to spend the night watching Carla DiDolche sleep? Why did she have to show up here, after all these years? And at a time when J. J. Sloane was considering whether or not to give Tobias the lease? Right now, he needed to concentrate, and he could hardly do so with Carla traipsing around the Sloane mansion in a nightgown. "See? It's just a piece of glass. Last time you were here we hadn't yet started using this room."

"I don't remember coming in here before," she admitted.

"It's a nice part of the building. Away from Fifth Avenue," he said. "Quiet."

Her eyes slid to the partition again.

His followed.

Before now, the room had never seemed so intimate. By rights, of course, he should have had a standard dream clinic facility, where glass walls separated observers and sleepers; because he'd been forced to convert the old mansion, he and his colleagues had settled on putting glass triparte panels near the beds. "We try to offer sleepers privacy while they're being monitored," he explained.

"I see."

So did he. In just a few hours, Carla was going to be tossing and turning under the covers. Knowing Carla, she'd manage to get the sheets, not to mention whatever nightclothes she'd brought, twisted around her waist.

He chewed the inside of his cheek. Yeah, from what

he remembered, Carla favored those little silk numbers that were calculated to drive a man crazy. Not that she'd have brought something like that here, of course. At least he hoped not. No, the staff always advised people to bring something comfortable and unrevealing. And yet...

Maybe it was too bad. As angry as he was with her—would always be with her—and as adamant about never rekindling their romance, Tobias had to admit he wouldn't mind having sex with her again. At least once. For old time's sake. Maybe he just needed to know that he could do it and walk away from her, the way she'd walked away from him. Gritting his teeth, he wished she hadn't shown up here.

After all, on a physical level, no woman had ever excited him as she did. She made his palms itch to touch, his mouth yearn to plunder. His eyes slid to her figure. Her body was so lush. All curves. Her breasts and hips were full. Back when they'd been together, she'd sometimes complained about her weight; for a week or two, she'd deprive herself of the incredible food her mother made, and the sweet, gooey, syrupy cakes they'd served in the café.

But Tobias had thought she was perfect. Soft, just the way a woman was supposed to be. Personally, he hated women who were so thin that you could see jutting bones, not that he'd been able to convince Carla of it.

Realizing a long silence had fallen, he said, "I think you should be comfortable here for the next couple of nights."

"Nights?" He could see her throat work as she swallowed.

"You really think it will be more than one?"

Just looking at her, he was sorely tempted to keep her here until his lease ran out. Given how his thoughts were progressing, and the way Carla kept dropping her gaze over him as if she, too, was fondly recalling their old times, Tobias had a sneaking suspicion they were soon going to wind up together in the four-poster bed.

So what if he'd nearly married her? Wasn't that past history now? Wasn't he over the pain and humiliation of that day? Not to mention over Carla? Wasn't that why he'd married Sandy? To prove it?

"Can your parents stay?"

She nodded. "They're here for two weeks."

He smiled. "Staying with you?"

At that, she grinned back. "That's why I came here. I needed to escape."

He eyed her. Even if they had sex, they couldn't do it at the mansion, he suddenly decided. Not with J. J. Sloane running around looking for excuses to give the lease to the Preservation Society. If J.J. caught him in bed with a patient, Tobias would be ruined. He shook his head to clear it of confusion. Was he really standing here, a foot away from Carla, planning to go to bed with her?

"So, I'll need to stay over more than one night?" she repeated.

"Probably."

"On the phone, they said they couldn't tell me much."

He tried to ignore the breathless flutter in her voice. And how good she looked. Prettier, he decided, than when he'd tried to marry her. Her hair was longer, past her shoulders, and inky-black corkscrew curls that he knew felt like satin spilled around her face, bringing out her rose complexion and making her round dark eyes sparkle. Summer had always suited her. She was the type of person who was always active, on her feet and moving—the trait seemed encoded in the DiDolche genes—but now she looked remarkably still. And beautiful...so damn beautiful. Coming to his senses, he realized she was waiting for some kind of response. "Hmm?"

"I was hoping that just one night..."

"It usually takes a couple. With something like sleep apnea or nocturnal eating, it's often just a night, but when dreams are involved..."

When his voice trailed off, she nodded. Years ago, she'd sit and listen to him talk about his work as no other woman ever had, her eyes attentive, the set of her soft mouth rapt. She'd enjoyed those talks, asking questions that even his colleagues wouldn't think to.

"It would be nice if you can help me," she finally said.

He hoped he could. "I'm glad you're doing this."

"And you're going to monitor me?"

He'd already said so. He nodded. "Yeah."

She looked nervous, but she ventured another smile. "When do you sleep, anyway?"

"I still catnap in the day." He was one of those people who was blessed—or cursed—by only needing a few hours of sleep a day. "Hopefully, we'll turn your nightmares into dreams, Carla."

"And if you can?"

"Many times, when we've changed the dream content, people report that nightmares never come back."

As her dark eyes widened, he fought the urge to

reach out and touch her. He knew firsthand how the nightmares had haunted her since she was a kid, and now he knew she was hoping that he could whisk them away with one night of therapy. He saw that look on the faces of many people who came to him, looking for a cure. "Seven years ago," he said, "our research hadn't advanced to the point it has today." Before now, he couldn't have done much for her. He wished he could offer more in promise, but he couldn't, so he simply remained silent.

She looked around again, slowly taking in an old-fashioned bedroom that was as hopelessly romantic as the rest of the mansion; salmon-painted walls were hung with discreet oils in gilded frames, mostly impressionistic landscapes and ocean views with sailing ships. Two wing chairs had been positioned on either side of a carved oak mantle, and just as downstairs, beaded lamps adorned small round tables. Carla's eyes trailed from an oriental rug that covered the polished hardwood floor to a four-poster bed stacked high with pillows.

Then she looked at the triparte glass partition again, as if judging the distance that would be between them tonight. Behind the glass were machines he'd monitor. "The room belonged to Marissa Sloane's lady companion," he said apologetically. "I'd have put you in the master bedroom, but J. J. Sloane claimed it."

"The room's gorgeous."

He nodded his agreement. "Yeah, it is," he said. And suddenly he wished he was anywhere in the world other than here, in a bedroom with Carla, especially one with so many nineteenth century frills. No, he really couldn't believe this was happening.

Carla had been having these dreams since she was a kid, and he'd been involved in dream research for a decade, so why did she have to show up now? And in the same week as J. J. Sloane?

Sighing, he told himself he could be a professional.

"Do you really think you'll lose the lease?" she asked as if reading his mind.

He shrugged. "I'm trying to be philosophical. But I do wish I'd waited a few more months before stumbling onto Cornelius Sloane's porn collection."

A smile tugged her lips. "I saw that in the newspaper." *The Pittsburgh Post Gazette* had run a picture of the secret room. "Must have been exciting."

"It was. I landed right on top of a life-size nude."

"Have you spent much time reviewing—" she paused with mock delicacy "—artwork?"

"Not really. A couple of days ago, during a meeting, Mar—" Cutting himself off, he decided he would rather not mention Margaret Craig, Sandy's mother. "The Preservation Society put some of the pictures on the boardroom table."

"You have a boardroom?"

"Dining room," he corrected. "We use it for meetings."

"Oh."

"Anyway, I hadn't seen the pictures for awhile. They're kept in the safe." He hated how heat was slowly suffusing his body again. It was bad enough that he was spending tonight with nothing but a piece of glass between him and Carla, but he hardly wanted to stand around discussing porn. "Guess ads are hotter. While you're here, one of the society members will probably take you downstairs to see them, if you want. Like I said, they're in a safe.'' He was loathe to admit it, but he added, ''It really is a worthwhile art collection.'' He was just afraid the pictures would wind up being hung in his dream clinic. ''I'll make sure you see them.''

''Thanks.''

Another silence fell, and when it turned awkward, Tobias said, ''I'd better let you settle in. Dinner's in a half hour. When you get downstairs, just about anybody can direct you to the ballroom. That's where we eat.''

''Great. I'll see you then.''

''I'll be at a staff table, but…''

Somehow, he wished she didn't look quite so relieved. ''Then I'll wave,'' she promised graciously.

''The food's nothing like your mother's.'' Or hers. When he thought of Carla's homemade cannoli, his mouth watered. Images of candlelit dinners followed, and suddenly, all the memories hurt. Why had she run back down that aisle? In a heartbeat, the question he'd never ask again was on his lips. In the past, she'd tearfully said she didn't know, but that had hardly soothed him.

He figured it was because of her dreams. Not that curing her tonight—if he could—would make a difference. It was too late now. Realizing they were still standing in the frilly bedroom gawking at each other, he said, ''See you downstairs.''

''Thanks,'' she said again.

Turning on his heel, Tobias headed down a red-carpeted hallway. When he reached the stairs, he gave in to the urge to look back. Her hands were on her hips, and she was staring at the partition, her dark eyes piercing through the glass as if she was imagining him sitting on the other side. He watched as she took a deep breath, seemingly bracing herself for the long night ahead.

He knew exactly how she felt.

3

"JUST IGNORE ME," Tobias suggested quietly as he fiddled with the monitors behind the glass partition.

Yeah, right. How was she supposed to do that? With a frustrated sigh, Carla snuggled deeper into the bed, wishing she'd brought shorts and a shirt to sleep in, instead of the new pajama set her girlfriend, Melanie, had given her for her birthday. Not that she wanted to think about Melanie at the moment, since she'd been one of Carla's bridesmaids.

Just sleep, she commanded herself. She tried to roll onto her side, which would have been more comfortable, but then she remembered the white tabs affixed to her head. "Drats," she muttered, glancing at the long, multicolored wires that spilled over the pillow and snaked toward Tobias.

"I know it's difficult," he murmured from just a few feet away. "You'll get used to it, though. Do you think you can sleep on your back?"

"I'll try."

"You usually sleep on your stomach, don't you?"

Every time he remembered intimate details about her, she found herself half hoping his memory was every bit as graphic as hers. "Yeah, I do." Just as he probably still slept stark naked.

As she squeezed her eyes more tightly shut, her

mind returned to the pajamas she was wearing. In her drawer, they'd looked like exactly what the receptionist had asked her to bring, something comfortable and unrevealing. Once she'd put them on, however, she'd realized that the bicycle style shorts, while definitely easy to move in, were also incredibly tight. The top wasn't, but the way the jersey fabric draped her torso didn't disguise her breasts at all. Because of the slender straps, she hadn't been able to wear a bra without making her concern obvious. Besides, she'd finally told herself, it wasn't anything Tobias hadn't seen before....

He was definitely looking at her. Earlier, she'd caught him, and now, with her eyes shut, she kept imagining him drizzling that syrupy brown gaze down the length of her body—over her breasts, to the soft protrusion of her belly, then to her hips and legs. At the thought, each inch of her turned warmer—until she considered tossing off the sheet that covered her, so he really could be tempted. Warmth slid between her legs, followed by a shower of tingles. Blowing out a surreptitious breath, she pulled the sheet higher, tucking it neatly beneath her chin. This was just too weird, she decided. She couldn't sleep with Tobias in the room, no way.

She opened her eyes.

He truly was gorgeous. He'd removed the sport coat and tie, rolling the sleeves of a blue chambray shirt just above his elbows. Before she could say anything, he smiled encouragingly from behind the glass. "Just keep trying," he urged in a gentle tone that suited his profession. Calculated to work on patients like a lullaby, his voice stroked her like a caress. "Everybody has trouble at first. It's hard to sleep while people watch.''

What was he thinking about her? she wondered as she shut her eyes again. Surely, it hadn't been easy to have her show up at the clinic. Her throat tightened. He was being so nice. And he didn't have to be. During dinner, she'd been impressed by how well-respected he'd become, too. Obviously, the clinic was hugely successful. All the staffers treated him with deference, and clearly loved his sense of humor.

So did she. After dinner, he'd wound up showing her around the building, since she hadn't been here for so many years, and she'd been astonished to find herself having fun with him and with the people he was treating. She'd dined with a vampirish night owl named Zeke Tanner whose pale complexion and black attire made him look as if he'd never seen the light of day; he was being treated for delayed sleep-phase syndrome. Seated next to Zeke was Lucy Jones, a housewife from the suburbs who'd fallen asleep twice while she tried to eat because she suffered from narcolepsy. And then there was a sweet elderly man, Mr. Clearview, whose REM behavioral disorder caused him to act out his dreams. He'd informed Carla that he didn't really care, but he often dreamed about fighting attackers, and last week, just before dawn, he'd accidentally given his sleeping wife a black eye.

Carla smiled now, getting drowsy. Yes, the clinic's patients were quite a crew. Unexpectedly, she'd felt some relief just from talking to the others. Hearing about their struggles, she didn't feel so alone. For the first time, she began to think maybe Tobias could help her. Maybe the dreams that haunted her really would end soon. In addition to bearing their burdens with grace and equanimity, the people Carla met had also given her countless ideas about how to improve the café. She shouldn't have been surprised. After all, who knew more about coffee than the sleep-deprived?

Sighing, she let her mind drift. Yes, Tobias was here in the room, but she had to forget that. She had to sleep. She had to let Tobias cure her....

As she drifted, her mind mulled over their after-dinner walk. Once alone, they'd been careful not to talk too much about the past. They'd simply walked around the mansion and its grounds, and as Carla began to dream, she imagined Tobias reaching over to twine his fingers through hers.

"Nice evening, huh?" he asked as her side brushed his.

Breathing in the complex scents of the summer night, she nodded her agreement as her eyes swept the landscape. "Beautiful."

Was she really here with the man she'd nearly married? A man she'd never thought would forgive her enough to share such a quiet moment? She'd felt like a princess as they walked across a thick emerald-green carpet of late-summer grass, hugging the interior perimeters of the high wrought-iron fence that separated the clinic's massive stone structure from Fifth Avenue. With its palatial columns and the stone swags that hung above French doors which, in turn, led to a wrap-around veranda, the place looked like a French castle. Inside, room after room bespoke the opulent grandeur of another age, with fabric-covered walls, breathtaking antiques and gold tablecloths laden with thick fringe. Golden August twilight, streaked with the pink fingers of the coming night streamed through floor-to-ceiling windows, adorned with sumptuous velvet draperies held back by gold ties.

The place was even more romantic than Carla remembered.

They'd wound up in the old dining room, and she'd been delighted when Tobias had shown her an old framed daguerreotype photograph of her building, dating from around 1880. Until tonight, she'd never known that the edifice where she lived and worked had been constructed by Cornelius Sloane, although it made perfect sense. At the turn of the century, when Pittsburgh was so smoky it was described as a two-shirt town, and when Sloane's mills were pouring tons of steel into the economy, Cornelius Sloane had been greatly responsible for providing the city's infrastructure.

Bloomfield, the Italian neighborhood where the DiDolches settled, was full of rowhouses and tenements designed to house immigrant workers. Carla's great-great grandfather, the first DiDolche to come through Ellis Island in New York and land in Pittsburgh, had come expressly to work in Sloane's mills. Instead, however, he'd opened DiDolche's.

Even today, the block of connected businesses on Liberty Avenue housed Gato and Gambolini's wine importing concern on the one end, and DiDolche's on the other. As she and Tobias could see from the picture, the row of buildings had been constructed at the same time, going up much like one of today's prefab units. Included were many small businesses needed to service the community. Like Gato and Gambolini's and DiDolche's, many of the others remained there today, even though most had changed hands. There was still a jewelry shop, a movie theater, a shoe shop and a hardware store. Each business had, as Carla's did, an apartment overhead.

For long moments, she and Tobias had stood next to each other in front of the picture, with her feeling dangerously aware of his presence—of the warmth seeping from his body and the heady male scent of his skin. Tension had snapped between them like fire-crackers in July, and she'd considered simply turning to him, to ask if he wanted to revisit old times. She didn't, of course. Instead, they'd only looked at the photo, letting the hazy yellow tones transport them to another age.

Her mind spiraling deeper down, Carla sucked in a sharp breath as she edged onto her side, barely aware now that she strained the white tabs glued to her scalp, along with the wires running across the floor to Tobias....

There was something disturbing about the photo-graph, she thought now. But what was it? As she stared into the picture, the streets came alive. Busi-nessmen in old-fashioned suits walked along Liberty Avenue, sidestepping horse-drawn buggies, carrying bags containing their second shirts, ones they'd don when they reached work since the smoke-choked skies would always ruin the first. Her breath quickening, Carla trailed her gaze over the building that was under construction. Unusual scaffolding formed a makeshift staircase that ran the length of the block, from the topmost floor of what would later become DiDolche's, to the ground floor of Gato and Gambolini's. Appar-ently, this allowed construction workers access to all the floors of the connected buildings. The block-long staircase must have been removed when the building was complete....

Suddenly, everything turned dark. Her pulse quickened. Her heart missed a beat, then slammed back into action, beating a fast tattoo against her ribs, making her breath shallow. Where was she? She looked around wildly, but she could see nothing, only impenetrable inky blackness. The air was stuffy. Enclosed. Cramped. Claustrophobia claimed her. She had to get out of here!

But she was trapped. Stairs ran every which way. Some went upward. Some down. Some sideways. But how could steps go sideways? That was impossible. Horizontal steps didn't exist....

Except in dreams.

She tried not to panic. Surely, she was just asleep. Surely, she'd wake up soon. Yes, that was it. She was sleeping and this was a very bad dream.

Wringing her hands in the darkness, she told herself to think, and yet she couldn't. If only she could force herself to wake up. Open your eyes! she told herself.

And then the image vanished. It was replaced by the dark room she'd seen so many times before. Or was it really a room, after all? Darkness faded into the corners, seeping against the walls, obscuring them. Hidden in the shadows, she reached out her hand and touched something metal and cold. What was it? Where was she?

And who was the man seated at the desk? Terror gripped her. He was huge and burly. His massive shoulders were hunched, so he could better see whatever was on the desk. An overhead light seemed to move slightly, accentuating the weak, watery beam that shined down on a head covered with what might have been black hair. But it was hard to tell. It was too dark, the illumination too faint to work like a spotlight.

She watched as he slowly lifted something. His beefy fingers, she realized, were hooked around the sides of a metal object. Gold glinted—just a flash of it—then she realized his index fingers were curled around a waistband. To golden underwear?

Nothing made sense. But slowly, gently, he lifted a pair of golden underwear higher into the air, and she could hear his breath catch in the dark with an emotion that felt sinister. She had to do something! Run! Wake up!

But she was rooted to the spot.

And then everything changed again. The man vanished, and now he was nothing more than hot breath against her neck and a raspy voice sounding at her ear saying, "If you marry, you will die."

Her pulse accelerated, ticking in her throat, making her feel weak from the adrenaline rush. The taste in her mouth was acrid, and sweat beaded on her forehead. She was desperate for this to end! Instead, the dream started over. She knew she'd never escape. She was alone in the dark again, wringing her hands. Stairs went upward. Downward. Sideways. She turned her head—this way, then that—but everywhere she looked, inky blackness stretched to eternity. There was no way out—

She felt a jolt.

What was that? It wasn't unpleasant...no, not at all. In fact, sweet relief seemed to slide through her body.

All at once, the dream was gone. There was no trace of the man or of the darkness that surrounded him.

Light filled her mind. The mustiness she'd previously smelled vaporized. Soft, sweet-smelling summer air infused her instead, tantalizing her nostrils and filling her lungs. An explosion of beautiful pastel colors followed—dreamy blues and lilacs. Translucent pinks and yellows that were the color of a gorgeous day's first rays of sunshine.

She felt another jolt, pushing pulsing electricity through her body. The pleasure was almost orgasmic. Her nerve endings hummed. Music played from somewhere far off. Close by, water gurgled, and in tandem with the sound she realized she and Tobias were on a bench in the garden of the Sloane mansion.

No…now they were standing. Everything was moving swiftly, the images disjointed, the way they so often were in dreams. One more little jolt of inexplicable pleasure zapped her. It was as if someone was injecting her with a drug designed for love. Slowly, she ran her tongue across her lips.

"Let's do it right here," Tobias said.

Eyeing him, she knew she wouldn't need much coaxing. At some point, he must have reached down, grabbed the hem of her new emerald-green sundress, and lifted it off, over her head. There was nothing beneath. She just so happened to be naked, which was going to work out quite well. Tobias's dreamy brown eyes closed to half mast, the gaze turning smoky with lust as it swept over her. Hers traveled down his bare chest, settling on his belt, then dipped lower where worn denim curved over an obvious erection, cupping him like a gloved hand. Just looking at him, knowing he was ready to love her, she felt her tummy jump.

"We shouldn't be doing this," she managed to say, her voice catching. They had a past, a history. She'd left him at the altar, after all.

But right now, he didn't seem to mind in the least. He tried to look innocent. "Do what?" he teased.

"Make love."

"Why not?"

"Because of what I did to you."

He merely grinned, his eyes flicking once more down her naked body. "I remember a lot of things you've done to me, Carla DiDolche," he said. "Leaving me at the altar was only one of them."

"But..."

Just as she started to offer some sort of apology, he silenced her with a deep, wet kiss. His mouth felt so impossibly good that it sent shivers coursing through her, racing through her limbs, settling at the core of her. All her nerve endings seemed to bunch into knots, and her lower belly felt as if it was melting into her thighs as he deepened the kiss, using his tongue to part her lips, time after time. Wonderful sweet scents from the garden mixed with something hotter, something more dangerously male. As he flicked his tongue with increasing urgency, gliding its silken side along hers, she forgot the past and responded, arching toward him and gasping as the smooth, long-tapered fingers of his hands glided up her rib cage.

"Touch me," she urged as the pads of those practiced fingers teased her, lingering just beneath breasts she wanted him to cup and knead. She wanted him so badly. Shutting her eyes tightly, she rode the sensation wrought by the kiss, and she dreamed about the coming minutes, when he'd be inside her, stretching and filling her.

And then the magic came. As he captured her mouth more firmly, locking his lips tightly over hers, he closed both his huge hands over her breasts. Using his thumbs, he circled the already taut peaks, roughing the tips, making then tighten even more. As he pushed her toward the edge, she moved her hips, cradling his as she rocked against him, making him moan.

He was still dressed, and as a blaze of fire raced over her, she damned the jeans that covered his lower half. Reaching a hand between their bodies, she continued kissing him, thrusting her tongue deeply as she slid a hand downward, then over the hard ridge beneath his fly. He was so long…so thick. Her heart hammered.

"Yes…yes," he panted.

"You're so ready," she whispered between kisses. So painfully, deliciously hard. Pushing out her chest, she offered her aroused nipples, and she could only suck in a quick gasp of longing and gratitude when he leaned back and angled his head downward. When the assault of his mouth began, she was totally lost. Blackness crowded into her mind, and she had no choice but to lean back her head in surrender. Over and over, she thrust her breasts for him…

He was panting softly. He gasped when her hand flexed on his jeans, closing firmly around his length. Sliding along the shaft, she explored every hot inch. Her thumb massaged ridges, her fingers, the head. She missed Tobias so much, she thought as she stroked him. Why hadn't she married him? Why had she run like a fool? What the hell was she scared of? "I've needed you," she moaned. "Needed this." He was supposed to be hers forever. Her husband, her lover. The man who shared her bed every night, and to whom she awakened every morning.

He was still swirling his tongue, the sensations unbearable. Just like she remembered…but better. Yes, so much better, she thought illogically, as his mouth closed hard on a bud. His tongue flicked the nipple like a vibrator, then he suckled deep, pulling the excited tip into his mouth until it seemed to rest against the pure wet silk of his cheek.

She was wet elsewhere, too. Shamelessly, she'd melted. She was dripping, her hips arched and begging. Her hand closed more tightly over him, feeling every inch of hot steel through the silken worn denim. Somehow, her shaking fingers pulled down the zipper, freeing him. Quickly, she pushed down his pants.

And then the jeans were gone. Suddenly, he was naked. She didn't know how he got that way, only that the dream fast-forwarded, and now he was standing before her without a stitch of clothes. He looked like a god. She'd forgotten how incredibly endowed he was. And how incredibly handsome. Or maybe she'd wanted to forget. Because if she'd remembered, she'd have had no choice but to drop everything and run to wherever he was. She would have begged him to forgive her for leaving him at the altar, just as he'd forgiven her in this dream. She would have asked him to please take off his clothes and let her…

Her eyes dropped hungrily. Time stopped as she took in every inch of a male body that just wouldn't quit. The male nipples were tight, like hers. The broad chest was covered in a tangle of yellow-gold silken hair that tapered, narrowed, and arrowed down to...

She shuddered as her eyes settled, then she slowly took in each nuance. He sprung from a nest of impossibly soft-looking curls—so big, so hard, so ready. A pinkened head was tipped by moisture, the shaft covered with ridges that promised to take her to a climax she'd never forget. Her mouth went dry, but only for an instant because he quickly leaned in for a kiss. His mouth, already wet, slammed hers....

And the image vanished. In a poof, it simply disappeared, and they were lying on a bed of grass so soft that it could have been velvet, or the silken strands of a mermaid's hair. They were shuddering and shaking, their skin damp, and Tobias was hovering over her. He raised himself on an elbow as he slid a hand between her legs saying, "You feel so good."

Whimpering, she cried out. "Oh, yes...please."

He'd been preparing her, making sure she was ready before he entered her, but now he paused to glide his hand over her folds. Using a finger, he opened the slit. "Oh," he moaned, his voice rough with need. "You're so wet."

She said nothing. She couldn't, not when he parted her once more, thrusting a finger deep inside her. Then another. But it wasn't enough. Her skin was glazed with heat, her mouth dry from panting. She wanted more. Him...inside her, not this maddening, teasing, thoroughly annoying finger that kept thrusting and withdrawing, then lazily traced circles over her clitoris. "No wonder I didn't marry you," she muttered in hopeless frustration.

He merely laughed. "Bothersome, aren't I?"

And how! Arching, she felt the fire inside her gather force. It was out of control. She was burning up! Every inch of her burned. Deep inside, she was aching. His thrusting finger seemed to touch her womb!

He had to stop.

Senseless words tumbled from her lips. She was begging him. But he wasn't going to stop, of course. No more than she was going to stop her own hand, which found his silken length once more and stroked until he gasped. "Tit for tat," she whispered, wanting him to give up...to make love to her, properly. I want you inside me, she thought. I need...

Please.

His finger was too much. She exploded. The sweet spasms of release were still rocking her when he knelt between her legs. Hot and smooth, the tip nudged her opening. She parted instantly, and he slid inside, each ridge pushing her back toward the edge she'd just visited. Yes. She was going to come again. Tobias was going to make her come and come, and never stop coming.

She closed around each thick inch as he pushed. Each glorious ridge caught on the insides of her slick tunnel, until he'd tossed her off a cliff, into a blissful state of joy she'd never imagined existed, not even with him...

And then she was simply riding him, moving and shaking, her legs wrapped tight around his waist. Her full breasts were bouncing, the taut tips brushing the silken hairs of his chest. He was loving every second, too. Shuddering, he curled his hands on her backside, his fingers stroking as he urged her up and down...

"Close," she whispered simply. So close. They

were both on the edge. She could feel him inside her...getting tighter, hotter. Until he was hovering above that hair-trigger place where just one more touch would make him...

Gasping, she knew he'd never been this hot. Just as she hadn't been this open. Bouncing, moving, thrusting. She was right there now. She cried out, her nails digging into his powerful shoulders.

Bouncing, moving, thrusting.

He groaned. She felt his hot stream shoot inside her. Oh, God, she couldn't stand another minute of this. She was letting go....

She was letting go....

TOBIAS HARDLY NEEDED monitors to tell him Carla was deeply aroused. The jagged lines that recorded her brain waves were definitely shooting to peaks and diving to valleys, but he could see from her face that whatever earthquake was exploding inside her was a six on the Richter scale.

Her body told the rest of the story.

Even though Tobias was thoroughly awake, he could barely concentrate on the dream-monitoring equipment. His every last nerve was zinging just like Carla's. For the past twenty minutes, he'd been as hard as a rock and fighting the urge to go climb into her bed.

"Dammit," he muttered on a frustrated sigh. This was impossible. How could he act professionally when Carla had just kicked off the covers? He watched, mesmerized, as her incredibly shapely legs slid on the mattress as if she was dreaming that she was wrapping them around his waist.

Surely, that's not really what she was dreaming.

"Pull yourself together." Tobias twisted a dial to send another jolt of electricity to her brain. Oh, yeah. The treatment was definitely working. Or was it?

He frowned. Probably, given the indicators before him, Carla was having one of her recurring nightmares when he'd begun zapping her. Usually, under these circumstances, the subject would continue the nightmare, but later report that some change in it had occurred. The monitors shouldn't have begun indicating that she was dreaming about sex.

"I wonder what it means?" he whispered, his thought purely academic until he lifted his eyes. They landed on Carla's tight T-shirt. His mouth dried as he took in the stiffened nipples pushing against jersey fabric. She seemed to be begging for his touch, for the warm, slick heat of his mouth. Earlier tonight, as they were walking in the garden, he could tell she'd missed him.

He sighed. Every time he looked at Carla, he felt as if warring emotions were going to tug him apart. Half of him wanted to stand, walk to the bed, and climb in with her. The other half could never forgive her for what she'd done seven years ago. Or now. He couldn't forgive her for coming here, either, and tying him in knots. Why couldn't she just leave him alone?

Returning his attention to the monitoring equipment, he blew out another sigh. Over the years, he'd done enough interviews with dreamers to know Carla was very definitely dreaming about sex. He'd love to see exactly what was going on in her head. Who was she with? Were they making love?

"Is it me?" he whispered, unable to stop a slight smile from curling his lips.

She twisted, pushing away the covers as if her internal temperature had soared to unbearable heights, then she moaned. As she tossed her head on the pillow, all those dark, slippery-soft curls looked stark under the moonlight streaming in through a window.

Suddenly, he just couldn't stand it anymore. Rising abruptly, he headed for the bed. Once there, he merely stared downward. With her so near, just beneath him, he could catch the sweet musky scent of her arousal rising from the mattress....

He groaned out loud. What was he supposed to do? Wake her? Get in bed with her? Sucking in a breath, he arched slightly, pressing his lower half to the mattress, wishing the folds in the covers were the soft folds of Carla's skin. Even though she was sleeping, she seemed to sense he was there, and when she turned her head on the pillow again, her chest thrust toward him.

Oh, yes, it was thoroughly unprofessional, but he really couldn't take it anymore. Lifting a finger, he traced it around her tight nipple. One little touch wouldn't hurt, right? He'd almost married her, after all. Ever so gently, he slid the pad of his finger to the bud; he watched in fascination as it constricted even more. Barely breathing, he tempted fate and rubbed one more very slow circle where she was so obviously aching.

She opened her eyes.

"I HOPE Carla's being helped," said Jenna, turning away from where she'd been arranging cakes in the case at DiDolche's. "She rarely admits the dreams are bothering her, but..."

"You know how Carla is," agreed Mary DiDolche. "She's headstrong, never complains."

"That's my girl," added her husband, Larry.

Mary shot her husband a smile. A heavy, buxom woman, she was wearing one of the long black dresses she favored. Her black hair was pulled into a bun. "Why aren't you eating with that espresso?"

Larry patted his belly. "Staying in shape for you."

Frowning, she tossed him a shrug. "Fitness programs," she griped derisively under her breath. Mary believed that man thrived on rich foods, especially desserts laced with cream.

"She's at the sleep clinic?" asked Vince Gato, who was seated at the counter, sipping his morning espresso. It wasn't really a question, since the reason for Carla's absence was common knowledge in the neighborhood.

Larry DiDolche shook his head. "Yeah. She says they have treatments that can turn bad dreams into good ones. I hope it works. My little girl's been having those dreams since she was three. Used to sleepwalk, too."

"Don't forget the insomnia," added Mary.

"Hey, when she's back home," Larry continued, "you'll come for dinner, eh? Nicco's down in the Strip District has been getting fresh fish that's out of this world. Mary's been cooking..."

"Ah!" she exclaimed. "I'll make veal. Forget Nicco's fish, Larry. It's the veal that Vince likes, right Vince?"

"You want the veal?" asked Larry, squinting.

''El perfecto,'' said Vince. Glancing beside himself, he took in the man he'd known from birth. They'd never really been friends, so much as friendly, since their family businesses had been housed on the same block for generations. ''You look good, Larry,'' Vince found himself saying. ''Retirement's treating you right.''

Larry's olive skin was tanned, and even though he was sixty-seven, he'd just started a new exercise training program. The black curly hair that he wore thrust back, off his forehead, was still full and thick, and his dark eyes danced like his daughter's. ''I feel better than when I was twenty,'' Larry reported. Chuckling, he flexed a muscle for his wife. ''A regular Italian stallion.''

Mary rolled her eyes.

Larry laughed. ''You oughtta come to Florida, Vince.''

''I've got the business,'' returned Vince. His sons had left home years ago, scattering to the four winds. He could only hope one would change his mind and return to run the store.

''There's Missy,'' Mary suddenly said under her breath, her eyes shooting daggers toward the plate glass window. On the other side, Mrs. Domico was letting her poodle sniff around the legs of the green bench.

''She's gotten a little better about cleaning up after him,'' offered Jenna.

Vince turned the conversation back to Carla. ''They think they can cure her, eh?''

Larry tossed back a sip of espresso, drinking from a tiny white cup decorated with the DiDolche logo.

"Yeah. Maybe now Carla won't have those dreams anymore."

"I sure hope not," said Vince. But what he was really concerned about were Carla DiDolche's hidden memories.

4

CARLA HAD SHOWERED and dressed in the communal bathroom down the hallway, and when she reentered the bedroom, Tobias was standing behind the glass partition, mulling over something he'd just scribbled on a legal pad.

He glanced up, and although he was smiling, the look in his eyes was veiled as if he didn't want her reading his thoughts or gauging his feelings. "Sweet dreams?"

And how! "Uh...the night was better than usual," she admitted cryptically, feeling a bit paranoid, wondering if he'd guessed at the content of the dreams he'd mentioned. As she returned the smile, he pulled out a chair for her and suddenly, tension snapped in the summer air; a clap of thunder sounded as if to announce it. Maybe there was no hope for the situation. Every time she and Tobias were within spitting distance, an invisible hand seemed to inject electricity into the space between them, supercharging it. Her body braced against it, her muscles tightening. For a second, a static image from her dreams entered her mind, like a snapshot. She could see Tobias, hovering over her, the bristly golden hairs on his legs brushing her shaking inner thighs as he moved between them, poised to enter her. In the next instant, she imagined him setting aside the legal pad, coming across the room and kissing her. Somehow, he seemed to read her mind, and simultaneously, they both inhaled audible breaths.

She pretended not to notice. Glancing through a window, she took in the darkening sky while heat that had nothing to do with summer made her body temperature rise. Billowing clouds rolled across the hazy sun like tumbleweed, changing into a phantom dragon, then a fancy teacup, then a unicorn. She looked at Tobias again. When their eyes locked, his still seemed veiled, making her wonder when the subject of their wedding would come up. With any luck, she could leave the clinic before it did. "'Morning," she finally said to him. "Looks like rain."

"Yeah. We need it."

She nodded. "I just talked to Ma. She said the weather's been great for business. As soon as they opened this morning, the shop was packed."

"That's good." His gaze followed hers to the window. "The garden needs it, too. Last night, I noticed the grass was starting to turn brown. I've been trying to conserve water, so we haven't been running the sprinkler as often this summer."

As she thought of how the garden had appeared last night in her dreams, she was with Tobias again, lying in the grass with soft petals falling all around them as he... Catching her thoughts, she squelched them completely.

"Here," he was saying. "Have a seat, Carla."

Next to him? "Now?" She looked at him, her heart fluttering, her eyes skating over him. Too bad the guy hadn't changed for the worse—gone bald or gray, or started to put on weight. As scrumptious as he looked, she simply couldn't stop wanting him, and after what happened at the altar seven years ago, surely he'd never want to get involved, not even for sex....

He'd never answered her question, was merely surveying her, so she added, "You look well rested." Luscious, too. He'd changed into fresh jeans and a very clean-looking white, button-down shirt. "When did you sleep?"

He shrugged, the expression in his eyes so penetrating that she wound up shifting from one foot to the other, feeling self-conscious. "After you did."

Yeah, those big brown eyes were definitely everything Carla remembered. Soft, warm and runny, like dark syrup over pancakes. "In here?" She glanced toward the armchairs near the fireplace. Somehow, the thought that he might have slept there unsettled her as much as the nearing proximity as she moved toward him.

"Nope. Down the hallway."

Lifting a hand, she smoothed her hair, tucking some strands behind her ears. She'd worn a pair of powder-blue pants with a matching T-shirt cross-stitched with tiny flowers, and she could tell he liked how she looked; the brief flash of heat in his gaze gave him away, as did the rest of his demeanor, how he absently licked his parted lips and leaned against the desk with feigned casualness as if there were tightly wound coils inside him ready to spring. Why had she run back down that aisle? she wondered for the umpteenth time. What sizzled between her and Tobias was undeniable. Except, of course, he'd never act on his impulses, she decided once more. Never. Not after what happened....

He nodded at the chair. "Why don't you plop your butt down?"

Because after last night's nocturnal excursions, Carla hardly trusted herself to get any closer. From two feet away, she eyed the monitors. "Just how much do they really tell you about what's going on in my mind?" she couldn't help but ask.

"Tons."

Great.

"C'mon," he said with another nod. "Sit."

She did so, then took a deep breath as he seated himself opposite her, scooting so near to the edge of his chair that their knees brushed. As he looked over some graph paper on the desk, she followed his gaze, taking in the jagged lines. "Those are my brain waves, right?"

He shot her a quick smile, just a slight lift of sexy lips that brightened this morning's dark day. "Yeah. In a second, after I take a closer look at them, I want to ask you a few questions about what you were dreaming, if you don't mind?"

Uh-oh. Images from last night's dream flitted into her mind again—a profusion of sweet-smelling flowers, then a rush of warm prickles that seemed to tickle her system from the inside; she recalled the look on Tobias's face as he'd entered her—his chin lifted, his eyes closed, moonlight streaming across a bare back that rippled like soft, dark water. "Uh...you want to ask me about my dreams?"

"If you don't mind," he repeated.

No way. "Shouldn't we go to breakfast? They only serve from eight to nine."

He glanced toward an old-fashioned clock on the mantle. "We've got time."

Wait a minute! She suddenly thought. Sucking in a sharp breath, she remembered Tobias standing over the bed last night. Was the memory real? Had he made love to her? Sometimes she had difficulty distinguishing dreams from reality, after all. That was one reason she'd come to the clinic. She frowned. Had she and Tobias gone outside together, to the garden? Or was it really a figment of her imagination?

She narrowed her eyes, searching his face for any hint of impropriety. If they'd really had hot sex last night, she'd note some sign of it, wouldn't she? Yes...she could swear he'd stood above her, and leaned down to caress her. She glanced at the bed and scrutinized the covers. Then she shook her head to clear it of confusion. She hated it when her dreams seemed so real! Desperately, she sifted through the images in her mind again, then mentally retraced the steps she'd taken last night, as she'd begun to dream. She'd been in that dark dank corridor where the stairs ran upward, downward and sideways. Had she taken a walk with Tobias before or after that...?

He glanced up from the papers. "Is something wrong?"

"Uh...nothing."

But still...she could swear he'd been standing over the bed last night, as if he'd been watching her sleep. Under the circumstances, Tobias wouldn't have touched her...would he? Perhaps not, but the event seemed even more real than her other dreams. Hadn't he thrust his hips against the side of the mattress, seeking relief from an arousal that had reached the point of pure agony? She shook her head. No...her dreams seemed real, she reminded herself again. And right now, she was confused by her own imagination, nothing more.

Propping the legal pad in his lap, he prepared to write. "Start from the top," he suggested. "Tell me everything."

Right, she thought. Maybe on a day when hell freezes over. "Everything?"

"Did you have the nightmares last night?"

Relief washed over her. She didn't mind sharing that information. "Yes."

He looked excited. "Any changes?"

Other than the fact that the nightmares segued into hot, sexy fantasies that involved him? "Uh...no." Feeling guilty, she added, "Not really, Tobias." Before he could continue, she glanced at the clock again. "Look, shouldn't we head down to breakfast instead? I'm starved. I'd hate to miss it."

"We will," he said on a distracted sigh. Ignoring her inquiry about food, he chewed his lower lip, as if perturbed.

Her heart softened as she watched him. He was truly endearing when he worked. Whenever he analyzed dreams, a layer of guardedness left his features. Despite his intense level of concentration, he looked almost boyish. "No changes in the nightmares?"

"None."

"But you definitely had them?"

"Yes. Just as I've always described them to you." Another clap of thunder sounded as if to punctuate her words, and she glanced toward the window just as the storm clouds darkened, turning the sky almost black.

When she glanced at Tobias again, she realized he thought she was lying. He scrutinized her. "Are you positive there were no changes in your nightmares at all?"

She met his gaze. "Obviously, you don't believe me."

He considered a long moment. "Dreams can be confusing...."

Especially when they involved making love to a man you'd almost married. "I couldn't agree more." But if she didn't say something to his liking, she was never going to escape the sharp gaze he was leveling at her. Nor was she going to get breakfast. Her stomach growled.

He shot it a glance, as if he was having a conversation with only that part of her anatomy. "We'll eat in a minute."

She sure hoped so. "Good. Ma would have a fit."

He smiled. "She likes to make sure people are well fed."

Like mother, like daughter. Taking a deep breath, Carla said, "Oh, wait a minute. Now, I remember." Tamping down her guilt, she let her mind race, then added, "I felt odd jolts of electricity." That much was true, but she'd prefer not to think about what followed, especially not now when her knees were brushing Tobias's and a four-poster bed was only a few feet away. He looked interested. "Jolts?" he murmured, half to himself. "Some patients report them. That was probably the impulses I administered to your system."

She nodded. "Yes, it was quite a shock," she

couldn't help but say. "And...and now that I think about it, the dream did change. I wasn't in the dark corridor. I was in the room with the man, and he was seated behind a desk. But just as he lifted the...you know..."

Perking up, Tobias scooted forward. "Golden underwear?"

Just as one of his knees settled warmly against hers, she managed a nod, cursing her awareness of him. "I..." Frowning, she wondered what on earth she should say next. "I started running then," she reported. "The next thing I knew, I was jogging through...uh, an enchanted forest." Hadn't he said some patients experienced that vision? She thought of the garden. "The flowers were blooming in pale colors, and it smelled like heaven."

"Anything else?"

"Not much. The important thing is that the dream changed, just as you expected. I was running through an enchanted forest and..." Pausing, she considered what to say next. "And eventually I lay down in a bed of flowers where I took a nap." With you.

"Really?" he said.

She nodded, then abruptly stood. "That's about it," she announced, mustering her brightest tone. "Now, how about some breakfast, Tobe?"

Tobe. She could have kicked herself for using his pet name. When he glanced up, he was clearly wondering why she'd done so. He eyed her for an amount of time that probably wasn't much longer than a heartbeat, but that felt like a full minute, and then he stood, too. Either he misjudged the space between them, or else he didn't care. Their lower bodies brushed, and as she registered the clean scent of soap and male arousal, he curled his hand around her elbow.

"Uh...Carla." His breath fanned her cheek.

Her throat seemed to close. All the supercharged kinetic air between them vanished as if sucked out by a breath. Melting brown eyes zeroed in on hers, and his mouth was just inches away. She was sure he was going to kiss her.

"What?" she managed to ask.

"About these dreams..."

She squinted, her eyes still riveted on a mouth that had twisted in the sexiest way. "What?"

"You're lying."

TWENTY MINUTES LATER, Tobias was sorry he'd forced the issue. Sure, the monitors had suggested sexual activity in Carla's dreams, but after making her describe them in graphic detail and realizing he'd been the object of her lust, he was about to come unhinged. It didn't help that, with the recollections, her cheeks flushed and her eyes brightened with barely hidden excitement. All he could do was ignore his own arousal and try to act professionally.

"Is going over this again really necessary?" she asked.

He was beginning to wonder. "What you're telling me doesn't make sense, Carla," he admitted. "Usually, when we administer electrical impulses, the subject's nightmare really does change. The changes are usually slower, too. There's not an abrupt shift to new subject matter."

Seemingly feeling sorry she wasn't a more predictable subject, she said, "Always?"

He chewed the inside of his cheek thoughtfully, then nodded. "This is the first time I've heard differently."

"Well...maybe I don't remember everything," she ventured. "Not everyone remembers their dreams, right?"

It was possible, he supposed. "Try to think."

She shook her head, frowning. He was glad to see her concentrating. Despite the fact that he'd apparently sent her hormones into total disarray, she knew he really was trying to help her. "In the dream, I was standing there..." she finally began.

Naked, he thought. With him. As she squinted her dark eyes, some of the embarrassed color drained from her cheeks, and he couldn't help but wonder what exactly she was seeing in her mind.

Probably, it was better if he didn't know.

"Just standing there?" he prompted, shifting uncomfortably in his seat, still trying to ignore the pang at his groin and hating his own sexual dyscontrol. Whatever Carla did to his male senses, she was still a patient...and someone he'd cared about, someone he'd known for over ten years. Sighing, he drifted his eyes over a powder-blue outfit that hugged her curves and made her look remarkably feminine. As she spoke, despite his good intentions, he caught himself imagining that he was unbuttoning her top with his teeth.

"The man was next to me," she said. "His breath sounded harsh as he bent down next to my cheek. He said, 'If you marry, you will die.'"

At the words, Tobias's chest tightened, and he pushed away the recollection of her running out of the church. "Right." He'd heard that part a thousand times before. "And then?"

"And then…just like I said—" When she raised her gaze as if for confirmation, he became aware of how physically close she was. He could hear her soft breaths, see the slight rise and fall of her chest. Once more, his eyes traced the powder-blue top, following the slopes of her breasts, catching hints of lace beneath the fabric. He saw himself flicking open a front catch of the bra and pushing the cups back. Gently, he lifted each breast, lightly squeezing, loving the weight in his hands.

She said, "In the dream, everything changes."

For a second, he had absolutely no idea what she was talking about. "Hmm?"

"Everything changes," she said again.

He managed to refocus his attention. "Suddenly?"

She shrugged as if wishing she could report otherwise, since what she was saying didn't fit with the pattern previously offered by other dreamers. "Yes. Like the snap of your fingers. One minute, I was in the nightmare…"

"And the next?" As he licked his lips against their dryness, he realized the truth: he wanted to hear every word of this again. In his years as a sleep expert, he'd listened to many wild dreams, but Carla's sexual odyssey was better than any *Penthouse* letter he'd ever read. Especially since he just so happened to be the star.

She exhaled, the color in her cheeks deepening once more as she continued, "Light filled my mind, like I said a few minutes ago. And I felt pleasure…"

His mouth went bone dry. Maybe this wasn't strictly

necessary, but he couldn't help asking. "Can you describe the pleasure?"

Her cheeks turned almost crimson. "It was like... uh...like an orgasm."

He managed a professional nod, then busied himself by writing something nonsensical on the legal pad. "Okay." Okay? his mind echoed. Had he really said that? Was he really sitting here with Carla DiDolche, discussing orgasms? Hell, maybe he was the one who was dreaming. At any second, maybe he'd wake up.

But instead, she continued, "That's when I heard what sounded like a waterfall. And you said, 'let's do it right here.'"

"Do it?" He couldn't help but prod, just wanting to hear her say it. "Do what?"

"Uh...make love."

"And you agreed?"

On the one hand, she looked as if she'd like to be anywhere but here, in this room, describing her erotic dreams to him. On the other, the pulse in her throat was ticking madly, as if she'd never been so excited in her life. "We already went over this once, Tobias."

True. "I just want to make sure I've got it right. Just hit the highlights." He really did want to have any material he might be able to use to help her.

She sighed. "I said we shouldn't be..." She paused delicately. "But you said you really wanted to..." She paused again delicately. "And so we began..."

"Having sex?" Just as he said the words, his gaze landed on the clock. Inwardly, he groaned. "We really are going to miss breakfast," he said, interrupting the interview. "We can continue after we eat."

As she stood, was it his imagination or did she really look disappointed? She said, "I guess we'd better go then."

He stood. Just as moments before, he'd forgotten how close they were. Recounting her dreams must have unsettled Carla because she startled and moved backward. Her heel caught the chair leg and instinctively, he reached to steady her. As soon as his hand curled around the soft, smooth point of her elbow, he knew it was a mistake. He felt breathless, dizzy. Her scent tunneled to his lungs with uncanny force. His groin was flush against her pelvis, and judging from the awareness in her widened eyes, she'd noticed. Fighting the urge to button his sportcoat, he offered a slight waggle of his eyebrows. After all, what did she expect? He was a professional, but she had been divulging fantasies worthy of a triple-X theater...

"Oh," she suddenly said. "I forgot."

He wished he wasn't overly aware of the steady thud of his heart. "You remember something else?"

"You know how I said we were near the bench in the garden?"

He wasn't sure he could stand talking about her dreams any more. "Yes." According to Carla, they'd been standing, and he'd just removed her emerald-green sundress. Didn't she know she was making him crazy with lust, just the way she had back in high school, when they were teenagers? He was barely aware of it when his hand was tightened around her elbow, or when he drew her an inch closer. He angled down his head, to hear her better. "We were, uh, naked. And standing..."

"After that, the image vanished. I forgot."

"And?"

"The next thing I knew, we were lying on a bed of grass."

Somehow, his eyes had settled on her mouth. It was red, soft and ready. He tried his best make his interest sound strictly clinical, but he was beginning to wonder if Carla was driving him wild intentionally. "Really?"

"We were shuddering and shaking," she continued. "Our skin was damp." Gazing up at him, she knitted her brows. "You said all this is important, right?"

He was being quickly reduced to a state in which he wanted to start begging. "Very," he forced himself to assure her. "At least if you want me to help you." That much was the truth.

She nodded. "I forgot to tell you I started whimpering, and..."

Any breath he'd had was now gone. "Whimpering?"

Looking thoughtful, she nodded once more, as if trying to recall what happened next.

All he could say was, "Like this, Carla?"

His mouth descended—swooping down, capturing hers, locking as tightly as a medieval chastity belt. Time stopped for just a heartbeat, then he plundered, thrusting his tongue deep. Her lips parted, allowing him access to the rest of the kiss, a fast, furious tumble. Like water bursting forth from a dam, its trajectory was fierce, beginning in a gushing explosion. As his tongue slid alongside hers, he could feel the heat of her skin radiating through her clothes, and he moaned, the natural force of the kiss quickly carrying everything to the next level.

Circling his arms around her back, he drew her closer, desire coursing through his veins when her full breasts cushioned against his chest. The tips peaked against his shirt, causing him to shudder. "Like this?" he murmured, soliciting a whimper from her as one of his big hot hands cupped her neck. Flicking his tongue to hers, he used his long fingers to slowly stroke her creamy skin, tracing from her collarbone to the sensitive space behind an ear, then driving his fingers deep into her hair, raking them across her scalp.

Oh, yes, Carla was definitely whimpering. Quick needy sounds energized the kiss, but as he thrust his tongue deeper, letting it go wild, he couldn't help but wonder what he was really doing. Oh, he wanted to kiss her until they were both so hot and bothered that they'd climb into the big four poster bed. After all, he'd loved this woman. He'd been ready to marry her and live with her until his dying day.

But now…

He forced himself to break the kiss. With her mouth still an inch away, looking so swollen and ruby-red and ripe, Tobias didn't know which was worse—kissing her or forcing himself to stop.

On one side was the heaven of the kiss. On the other side was the hell of what she'd put him through seven years ago. Ever since she'd walked back into his life, he'd considered loving and leaving her, just the way she'd left him.

But now, with her panting breath stirring his cheek, he wasn't so sure he could handle it. No doubt, he could reduce her to a physical mass of pleasure. He could use his tongue to make her writhe, or settle his mouth over the heart of her until she bucked with joy. He could enjoy her for hours until she was crazy in love with him again….

But then, he just might go crazy himself in the process.

"Whoa," she whispered. "What did we just do, Tobias?"

He considered. "Something we're going to forget."

She looked dazed, the lids of her dark eyes lowered, the irises as hot as sunshine in August. "Forget," she repeated.

"I think that would be a good idea," he agreed.

But how could he really forget the feel of her in his arms again, or how the nip of her waist curved under his splayed fingers, or how her gasps of pleasure sounded to his ears? Heat seeping from those powder blue pants was still showering him with tingling want.

A clap of thunder sounded again. As the skies opened and rain began slashing the window panes, Carla said, "It's going to be quite a storm."

"Yeah," he managed. But while he appreciated her effort to put the conversation back on track, it was nothing like the storm she'd just started inside him.

CARLA WAS SLEEPING.

As he watched her, Tobias exhaled a frustrated breath. This whole day had been a relentless hell. It was bad enough that the Preservation Society was trying to butter up Sloane Junior, but because he had to work, Tobias couldn't spend the same amount of time arguing his own case. After all, Carla was only one of his twenty-seven patients. Because the storm had knocked out power lines in the suburbs, as well as prompted a traveler's advisory, the clinic had run into staffing problems. Until two hours ago, Tobias had to assign someone else to Carla.

He should have been relieved. She'd avoided him at meals, and tonight, once she'd climbed into bed, she'd immediately squeezed her eyes shut and pretended to be asleep.

"As if I didn't know better," he murmured, his eyes taking in the machine gauges. Just a few moments ago, she had the nightmares, and just as before, he'd sent electricity through the wires attached to her scalp. Raptly, he'd watched the brain waves change patterns. Now, there was no denying that Carla was dreaming about sex again.

Probably with me.

He pushed aside the thought, as well as the urge to go to her bedside. Forcing his attention back to the monitors, his eyes followed the wild peaks of her brain waves, then the plummeting nosedives. Were they lying in the grass again, surrounded by flowers? Was she whimpering as she had today when he'd kissed her?

The kiss had left him edgy and tense. Not to mention confused about how to proceed. He was right to walk away, of course. After all, the woman had trampled his heart seven years ago.

But now…

He cursed as she scissored her uncovered legs. She had great legs. Muscular and yet womanly, with slender thighs and calves that curved like an undulating alpha wave. Her skin was so smooth. It would be as soft as velvet if he ran the tip of his tongue from her toes all the way up to…

He could almost taste her. Today, he could have easily swooped her into his arms, deposited her in the bed and made love to her. But could he walk away?

"You have to be sure you can," he murmured, his eyes lingering where her breasts stretched the nightshirt. Her nipples had stiffened, making the fabric pucker in tufts. He wanted to close his mouth over one and suck until she was panting.

But could he walk away? he wondered again, his eyes traveling down to rest on the mound so lovingly cupped by her pajama shorts.

"Sure," he suddenly whispered. Oh, this morning he'd been conflicted. But the more he thought about it, he didn't see why he couldn't have sex with her, then walk away. As if to convince himself, he whispered once more, "Why not?"

5

DON'T OPEN YOUR EYES. That was Carla's first thought the next morning. Feeling groggy, she snuggled into the covers, grunted softly, then rolled onto her side. As the gentle tug of the wires attached to her head further awakened her, images from last night's dreams filtered into her consciousness. She and Tobias had been on a trip they'd planned for their honeymoon, a cruise to the Virgin Islands.

"To my wife," he murmured, pouring flutes of bubbly.

"To my husband."

Their eyes meeting, they'd toasted, clinking their glasses before enjoying the cool effervescent taste. The evening sky over the ocean was shot through with rainbow colors, and the red globe of sun was dipping low, about to sink beneath the horizon line; the last vestiges of twilight touched the undulating waves surrounding them. Salt was on the breeze, mixing with scents of love.

"It's so nice out," she'd murmured.

"Beautiful," he'd agreed. "You are, too."

Setting his glass aside first, he did the same with hers, then he stretched an arm around her waist, pulling her into his arms, so she was in front of him. As his hands clasped over her belly, she curled her fingers around the smooth wood of the ship's railing and stared out to sea, sighing as his groin connected with her backside, flooding her with sweet sensations, the heat of the touch mixing with the emotions of her heart. He pressed his lips into her hair, peppering the strands with kisses before his warm, gentle fingers pushed them away from her face; his mouth settled on the length of her neck, delivering one long unbroken kiss that turned warmer and wetter as it swept in swirling arcs to her collarbone.

"Maybe we should go back to the cabin," she suggested huskily.

As heat infused her body, Carla scissored her legs against the sheet, getting more comfortable the deeper she sank into the covers. Suddenly, she frowned. Wait a minute! Her legs were uncovered. She was naked! Startled, she slid a hand from the pillow to her chest to check the state of her clothes.

But no... Relief washed over her. She was still in pajamas. Uncovered, though. Vaguely, she felt sure something had happened last night...something, well, significant. The air conditioner was humming; it had cooled the room, turning it clammy. Slitting open her eyes, Carla realized she was faced away from the glass partition. Was Tobias still here? What time was it? Her eyes shot to the clock on the mantle. Only five. That was good. There was still plenty of time until breakfast.

Yesterday's storm had passed and grainy gray light was starting to seep into the room, arriving in faint fingers of illumination that poked through the white gauze curtains. She stretched, raised her arms above her head and yawned, then she startled once more, her eyes widening. Was Tobias in bed with her? He had gotten into bed with her last night, hadn't he? They'd made love, right?

Oh yes. Shutting her eyes again, she registered the well-loved feeling of her body...the sheen of dried perspiration coating her skin, the pleasantly bruised feeling of her breasts, the slight stickiness between her legs and the warm tingling that she now remembered he'd left there with his touch....

Realizing she was holding her breath, she slowly, shakily exhaled, muffling the sound with the pillow. The whole incident was now as clear as a bell. How had it slipped her mind? It had happened earlier this morning, at probably two or three. She'd been dead to the world when she'd sensed movements beside her. Just as she'd glanced over her shoulder, he'd drawn back the covers. Blinking rapidly in the darkness, she'd barely been able to pinpoint his exact location. Just as now, she'd felt the room's cool air on her skin—but only for a moment because he'd slipped next to her, already naked. Right before the fronts of his thighs hit the backs of hers, she'd felt curly hairs teasing her skin; the hairs of his chest flattened against her back as he circled his arms around her waist, hugging her close, huskily murmuring naughty nothings that sent shivers through her as his groin connected with her backside. When his lips found her neck, they'd felt firm and cool, at least until he'd quit nibbling the space beneath her ear and begun kissing her in earnest, and the temperature had begun to climb....

"Is that you, Tobias?" she'd croaked sleepily. As if it could be anybody else.

"Nope."

She'd chuckled. "Oh, it isn't, huh?"

As he shook his head, strands of blond hair swept her cheek. It had been so long since she'd been held by someone she really wanted, she'd thought. By him. Over the years, she'd had dates, of course, and she'd come close to having sex, but the sorry truth was, this man had ruined her for every other. Every time she was about to make love with someone she thought she liked, she'd think of Tobias. As much as she hated to admit it, her mother was right. Carla never would stop loving him….

"Nope," he'd said again, whispering into her ear between kisses. "Who's Tobias?" he joked. "I'm the sandman."

She'd chuckled. "Too bad I was already asleep."

"Not really," he'd argued. "The sandman can give you so much more than pleasant dreams."

"Go ahead," she'd said. "Wow me."

Now warmth thrummed through her system. It strummed her insides like an invisible hand playing a guitar. Her nerve endings were singing. Yes, last night Tobias had treated her to the most delicious lovemaking of her life. It was even better than what they'd shared in the garden. Besides, that was only a dream. Last night, by comparison, had been a dream come true, a truly sizzling reality. She simply couldn't believe he wasn't angrier about what she'd done to him in the past….

"Tobe?" she whispered.

No answer. She frowned. Surely, he was still in bed with her. Surreptitiously, she glided a hand along the mattress, letting it creep toward the other side of the bed. He was gone. Disappointment welled within her.

It would be awfully nice to start the day with a repeat performance of last night, especially since she'd had such difficulty getting herself out of bed the past two mornings without her own specialty turbo coffee.

Her smile broadened. No, she really couldn't believe Tobias was being so nice. Last night—or early this morning, depending on which way you wanted to look at it—Tobias hadn't even mentioned the wedding. Apparently, he'd decided to let bygones be bygones and enjoy a hot, steamy one night stand.

Would he come back for more? Would it turn into an affair? Her heart lurched. Or something more? An image of his folks flashed into her mind, then a wave of guilt. The Frees had loved her, just as her parents had adored Tobias, but she hadn't seen them for years. If she and Tobias started sleeping together and enjoying each other's company, would a relationship evolve? If so, was she ready? Could she handle it this time?

Or would she blow it?

Again.

After all, the nightmares had returned. Despite Tobias's talents, she wasn't cured. Even now, with the morning light sifting into the room, looking as fine as baking flour and reminding her of the powdered sugar on the cakes she was usually signing for at this hour at the café, Carla could remember the sensations she associated from the dark dreams and feel the man's hot breath on her cheek as he said, "'If you marry, you will die.'"

She bit back a groan of frustration. Who was he, anyway? And why hadn't the electrical impulses Tobias had administered worked the way they usually did on clinic subjects? Why hadn't something in the nightmares changed? If only the man would turn around, maybe she really could confront him and be freed of the past. How could someone as hardworking and otherwise rational as herself be ruled by her own unconscious? The man's words were an empty threat. The man, himself, was only a phantom of her imagination. And yet when she thought of the last second of the dream—of his hot breath, the gravelly roughness of his voice, the warning—she wanted to crawl inside her own skin and hide forever.

It really had been enough to make her run from the altar. Oh, she'd told herself countless other things—that she was still too young, or that she wasn't really ready. But she'd loved Tobias, could love him again....

He'd wanted her so much last night. They'd had sex for hours! Nothing wore the man out. But now...how should she handle the morning-after awkwardness?

Taking a deep breath, she rolled over and realized the electrodes were still in place; he must have put them back on after they'd made love. Tobias was standing behind the partition. He looked under-slept and sexy, his usually straight blond hair tousled. Just looking at him, she had a sudden visceral memory of how the silken baby-fine strands had felt as they'd fallen between her spread fingers. She took in an untucked green button-down shirt so wrinkled that he could have slept in it, and his rumpled jeans. "Too bad you got dressed," she murmured.

Glancing up from the monitors, he grinned. "Hmm?"

"Nothing." She grinned back, then glanced toward

the closed door. Vaguely, she remembered him locking it last night. ''Why don't you come back to bed?'' she suggested, her voice barely more than a whisper.

In the long pause that followed he merely eyed her, seemingly liking what he saw. As his leisurely gaze burned down every inch of her, she tingled just as surely as if she'd been touched by his hand. ''Back to bed?'' he said.

Was it her imagination or had he put the emphasis on the word back? Frowning, she wondered if she'd been wrong. She really did sometimes confuse dreams with reality....

But no, she must have been right. He was circling the partition now. Hungrily, her eyes raked down the front of him as he moved. His bones and muscles seemed so fluid, just as they had back in high school, when he'd run on the track team. He stopped beside the bed, and when his thighs hit the mattress, he stared down at her, the outline of his body muted in the hazy early-morning light. He watched her take the electrodes from her head one by one. His voice was husky. ''Uh...you sure?''

''After last night?'' Arching an eyebrow, she sent him another smile of warm invitation. ''Absolutely.''

He hesitated briefly, then unbuttoned his shirt and shrugged, letting it roll from powerful, rounded shoulders. As it slid down his long smooth arms, she flicked her gaze over the coils of veins, then strong hands that looked huge and dark in the muted light; as the shirt dropped, her throat tightened. His jeans were already unsnapped, the bulge of his masculinity unmistakable. ''Climb in,'' she offered raspily, barely able to believe any of this was happening, her mind racing with the events of the past two nights. "Am I dreaming?"

"Let's see." Reaching down, he lightly touched her cheek in what was more a caress than a pinch. "How's that feel?"

She pushed the sheet further back. "Other things might feel better."

As he cracked a lopsided smile, a hank of blond hair tumbled down, falling across a sparkling brown eye. "I take it, that's a hint."

She chuckled throatily. "If I hint any harder, it's going to get pretty graphic."

His smile widened. "I like graphic."

"Then what are you waiting for, Tobias?"

When another look of indecision crossed his features, her cheeks warmed. What if he rejected her? But then, why would he? Last night, he'd made clear he wanted her, at least physically.

Just as she was beginning to doubt her perceptions, he slipped out of his shoes and got into bed next to her, wearing his jeans.

"You're still dressed," she complained, easily wreathing her arms around his neck. As images from their previous night's lovemaking flashed through her mind again, she shamelessly pressed the front of her body to his. "And I was counting on a repeat performance." She smiled against his shoulder since, judging by the bulge beneath the fly of his jeans, Tobias was more than ready to oblige her.

"REPEAT PERFORMANCE?" Tobias murmured, knowing he should feel guiltier as he scooted closer. As near as he could tell, Carla really thought they'd had sex last night. Which meant she'd had more erotic dreams. Considering what she'd already reported, he'd give his right arm to hear all the juicy details. He hedged. If he told her their lovemaking was a figment of her imagination, he might ruin their chances of starting the morning right.

"I...uh...do hope I can live up to last night, Carla."

"I don't think you'll have any trouble, Tobias."

"You don't, huh?"

"No way, baby."

Her throaty morning-voice caught as she spoke, and the sound grasped onto his every last nerve. As she rolled to face him, he squinted, getting a better look at her in the faint light; she squinted back, looking hazy, like a figure in one of the old daguerreotype photographs on display downstairs. Cupping his hands over her shoulders, he angled his head down for a kiss, the guilt vanishing as he did so. He wanted her. Right here. Right now. Even if he had to tell a little white lie to accomplish it....

But then guilt niggled once more, just like that.

And just like that, he tamped it down.

"Somehow," she murmured just before his lips claimed hers, "I think this might even be better than last night."

No kidding. He had no idea what she'd dreamed, but he was as hard as the steel Cornelius Sloane used to manufacture by the barge-load. What man wouldn't be? For the past half hour, he'd been watching Carla sleep, his eyes riveted to her sexy little nightshirt. Now, as he settled his mouth on hers once more, he felt a last, unwanted tickle of guilt.

He hadn't been in the room last night at all, much

less made love to her. Due to staffing problems caused by the storm, he'd been called to other duties, leaving one of his colleagues to monitor the machines and administer the electrical impulses that had apparently turned Carla's nightmares into erotic fantasies. He'd shown up here about a half hour ago, and he'd gotten the report on Carla's nocturnal activities.

He didn't really understand it. She was the first dream subject to respond this way. Not that he cared at the moment. Slipping a hand under the hem of the nightshirt, he pushed the soft jersey fabric over her breasts, catching the even softer flesh from beneath as he did so. Closing his fingers over bunching material and mounds of creamy skin, he groaned.

"I missed this," he admitted, squeezing gently, reveling in the sound of her satisfied sigh. "Here," he urged huskily, pushing the shirt the rest of the way over her head, then leaning back to settle his eyes on her naked upper body.

"You did?"

He had no idea what she meant now. The moment had captured him completely: the filtered light in the old-fashioned room, the heat already starting to rise on Carla's skin. "Did what?"

"Missed this?"

More than he wanted to acknowledge. "Oh, yeah." He nodded as he dipped his head for another kiss. Gently, he probed open her mouth, using his lips to part hers, waiting a minute, then dipping his tongue into the open slit. The kiss was long, slow, and not too hungry. Nice, he thought. Very, very nice.

She tasted sweet in the morning. Not quite peppermint, but definitely not morning breath, either. Just sweet, the way he remembered her tasting years ago. She looked pretty in the pre-dawn hours, too, he thought as he drew back, still narrowing his eyes in the faint glimmer.

She was smiling, her eyes at half mast, her long black eyelashes—a DiDolche trademark—creating spiky shadows on her rosy cheeks. Even half shut, her eyes were shiny and bright, alight with excitement. Yes, Carla possessed every trait that traditionally made so many Italian woman beautiful, he thought, his eyes trailing lazily over the wildly tousled curls falling on her face. Lifting his hand from a breast, he caught one of the curls between his fingers; tugging the string of black ribbon, he used it to bring her mouth to his again.

"Caveman," she whispered.

He chuckled. "I'm hardly dragging you off by the strands."

"I know exactly what you're doing." She rolled her eyes because he was touching her breast again. "And it feels so good."

He couldn't help but smile. "As good as last night?"

"Better," she pronounced, her voice as sexy as the light: soft, low and grainy.

As he continued caressing her breasts, he kept his eyes on hers, dark brown irises locking into dark brown irises. He glanced down. "Your breasts are perfect," he couldn't help but murmur. He felt like a fool for saying it, but he'd dreamed of seeing her like this; besides, it was true. She was full and ripe, and stroking the heavy, silky mounds of flesh made his mouth water. Her skin was so gloriously dusky in the early morning light, the creamy color of the lattes she served at the café.

With the same stealth as the slowly encroaching morning, need was overtaking his system. Her scent knifed to his lungs, his blood quickened, the pang at his groin became insufferable. Sucking in a shaky breath, he settled his gaze on nipples that were the color of wet sand. Sliding long fingers over the cresting tops of both breasts simultaneously, he closed his fingers, released them, closed them again.

Her breath caught, and the quick sharp inhalation further fueled his desire. Carla had always loved breast play. So did he. His slow strokes speeded until he was repeatedly strumming the reddening, erect tips, flicking them until they were astonishingly taut...until she was starting to strain her hips against him. After what she'd done to him in the past, he couldn't help but enjoy the power he so clearly had over her now. "I know how to touch you, don't I?" he urged, his voice dark and suggestive.

Her eyes might have been mere slits, but they were open enough to communicate smoke and heat. Yeah, he thought, the two of them were definitely about to start a fire. Was that really what he wanted? After all, he could get up right now, call it quits, and not risk falling for her again. He might even enjoy the shock on her face when she realized he'd aroused her only to leave.

She said, "You're good at seduction."

"Better at satisfaction."

"I remember."

Yes, he was definitely in bed with the woman who'd broken his heart, and maybe he would have changed his mind about it, but he registered the tight, constricted bud he was rolling between his thumb and index finger and simply said, "Me, too."

She shuddered. "Kiss me, Tobias."

He wasn't proud of it, but he had a flash fantasy of taking her right to the brink of orgasm, watching her pant, writhe and moan, and then getting out of bed and walking away. Even if he didn't do that, he definitely wanted to make Carla DiDolche beg. Yes, he was going to enjoy every second of it, moments from now, when she was consumed with lust. "Maybe."

"Why wouldn't you?"

He arched an eyebrow. "Are you going to kiss me back?"

"I don't know. Kiss me first," she said. "Find out."

Pushing his tongue between her lips once more, he let the kiss deepen with intention. Her tongue slid over his, then the pointed tips met and danced together. Moments later, that same unbroken kiss had turned urgent, hotter and wetter, just shy of sloppy. Deep and openmouthed, the thrusting of their tongues were starting to mimic the motions of hips that cradled together and began to rock.

"We used to like this in the morning," she gasped.

"We still do," he couldn't help but point out, offering a low-voiced grunt of longing as her pelvic bone connected with the bulge beneath his zipper.

She was panting softly, the sound shooting a spray of heat into his veins, pooling in his belly, warming it way down low and further strengthening a need he couldn't deny. Any questions about what he was doing here were long gone. What was about to happen next was inevitable. Splaying his hands, he pressed his fingers down her rib cage, then pushed upward once more, until her breasts were both in his hands again. Molding his fingers around the curves, he pressed them together, buried his face in the cleavage and squeezed.

She whimpered.

His groin tightened painfully, his erection bold and insistent. His body was begging for release as he found her mouth and sent the dizzying kiss soaring upward. "Italian spice," he whispered.

"Like Emeril."

"Who?"

"You know, the cook on TV."

"Oh, right. But I hope you're not. He's a guy."

"Whatever," Carla muttered, her husky voice tinged with annoyance, as if to say they had many better things to do than talk. And then imitating Emeril, she said, "Let's kick it up another notch."

"Bam," he whispered back.

His tongue gained speed then, flickering against hers like a flame before a breeze. Hot and vibrating, he used it to bring hers into play, and testing the weight in his palms, he lifted a breast, raised it high and kneaded the flesh roughly until she cried out, the jolt of sound making his body tingle.

"Kiss me," she murmured again, and he let her urge him on, his tongue getting away from him, moving wildly in her mouth while hers responded—flicking, gliding, licking.

She gasped, startling distractedly as he broke the kiss, the sound begging him to resume. He did, but when his mouth came back down, it locked onto a nipple. Moaning, he savored the feel of it between his lips. Deepening the kiss, he circled the stiffened tip with his tongue.

Seven years, he thought. Had it really been that long since he'd tasted her? Maybe...but he'd know the taste anywhere, this maddening brand of salt and honey. Up close, no matter how many days she'd been away from home, Carla DiDolche's skin carried the scent of coffee. Whether it was because she worked around the stuff all day, or because it was simply in her blood, he didn't know, but as he inhaled, he was stunned at what the scent did to him. That, and how it mixed with the deeper, more electrifying scents of her sexuality. It had been seven long years since he'd kissed her and now, the more he did, the seven years felt closer to a century. How had he lived without this?

Tremors were moving beneath each inch of her skin, and her hot, greedy little hand, with its trim manicured nails was slowly sliding between them. He breathed in sharply as her fingers rippled over his ribs, then gasped as her palm flattened and glided over his navel. Now, his heart was hammering, his breath shallow with anticipation. When she molded her hand over the most intimate part of him, applying just the right amount of pressure to make the caress feel heart-stopping, he lifted his mouth from the tip of her breast, knowing he was about to explode.

"A condom," she whispered.

Glancing up at her, he bit back a curse. He was so damn breathless, his chest as tight as his blue jeans over this truly uncomfortable erection. A condom. "I didn't think that far ahead."

She was so sexy, her hair even more disheveled than

when she'd awakened, and the expression of her half shut eyes was dazed. She was just as hot as he was. Squinting in confusion, she said, "What did we use last night?"

He felt the bulge pressuring his fly, then he felt the heat seeping from her pajama shorts. It was hardly the time to tell her they really hadn't had sex, that she'd only dreamed it. "Uh, we used..." It or them? he wondered. How many times had she imagined they'd made love?

"Oh, no," she murmured.

Lowering his mouth to her breast once more, he replaced a finger where his mouth had been, pinching the erect nipple, tweaking it, rolling his thumb around it. Glancing up again, he watched with satisfaction as practical matters so very obviously fled from her mind. Not that he'd have sex with her without a condom. It was bad enough they were in bed again after seven years. But the idea of Carla winding up pregnant with his baby...

Carla shut her eyes, thrust her chin upward and simply took the pleasure as he continued fondling. "There are other things we can do," he murmured.

"You always could think of something."

Indeed. Skating his mouth downward, he kept the tip of his tongue erect as he flicked it into her cleavage. He kissed a line further down, bisecting her ribs. By the time he reached her navel, she was arching, the flimsy fabric of her pants no barrier for the sweet heavenly scent of her sex that rose to greet him. Moaning, he traced the tip of his tongue around her cute little dip of a belly button. Circling it, he dipped a wet kiss inside, exploring the rim as he curled his fingers over the waistband of her bottoms.

Just then, a long, lovely arm stretched down, her fingers grabbing the tab of his jeans zipper. Gasping, he rolled away. He was about to explode. Sucking in another breath, he yanked the zipper over his erection, wincing at the painful movement. Pushing the pants down his hips, he tossed them and his briefs to the floor, beside his shirt.

She was next. A whimper was torn from her lips as he hooked his hands inside her waistband and pulled her pajama shorts all the way down her shapely, silky legs, then rubbed his palm briskly over her panties, warming the already hot mound.

''Red,'' he muttered simply, feeling as if he were going out of his mind when he looked at the panties; they were everything a man would want to see a woman wear at a moment such as this: silk, lacy and the color of a fire engine streaking through town during a five-alarm drill.

And she was wet. Oh, so wet. When his hand tightened on the lace, pulling the fabric into a fist, he realized she was drenched. So he tightened the fist another notch, making the panties taut, making them chafe against where she was most sensitive. Once she was writhing, he slid a finger under the leg band and pulled the panties all the way down. Leaning closer to her, he moaned. God, he loved the way women smelled. Especially Carla…

She scissored her legs, just as she did while sleeping, but now in nervous anticipation. He didn't blame her, either. He was about to drive her crazy. Letting her feel the hotness of his breath on her inner thighs, he smoothed his palm over her twitching, jumping belly. But there was no calming her, not really. So he planted a slow, wet scalding kiss on her inner thigh, gliding a hand under a crooked knee as he did, using it to push her leg higher.

"Open for me," he said, his barely audible voice sounding hoarse to his own ears, laced with passion.

Her rapid anticipatory breaths came quicker and she did as he asked. Leaning, he used the pointed tip of his tongue to trace spiraling circles on her other thigh, letting the kiss climb high...then higher...until he was tracing the groove where the leg band of her panties had been. Until she was squirming, panting and parting wider.

That's right, he thought. Beg me. Her every silent movement said she couldn't stand this a second longer. "Let me hear you, Carla," he whispered.

And she did, offering a sigh, then a high-pitched whimper as his tongue inched just a fraction higher, the pressure of it near her vaginal folds. She was so open for him. Like a flower.

He simply covered the heart of her. His whole mouth settled where she wanted it, and she uttered a long shuddering cry of ecstacy as he slid a hand between her and the mattress, lifting her, forcing her to arch for his lips, knowing that each new time she stretched for his mouth, she was coming that much closer to release. Once more, he had the flash fantasy that he could make her turn wild in his arms, under the ministrations of his mouth, then simply walk away....

But he knew he couldn't. Not anymore. Not when he was tasting the honeyed heat at the heart of her, not when she was exploding in sensations beyond her control. His fingers came into play, opening her further still, so his tongue could trail a long blazing line of fire. He pushed back the hood over her clitoris, the way she'd taught him years ago, and then his tongue was simply vibrating, the tip endlessly pleasuring her....

She gushed, drenching him with a burst of taste that nearly sent him over the edge. Not that he'd stop. No, he meant to go all night. He wouldn't let her rest. He wanted her to be sorry about the way she'd hurt him. He wanted to give her—in the taste of their bodies—a taste of what could have been....

Maybe she did, too, because she was shifting on the mattress, turning her body around, so that she could...

Gasping, Tobias threw back his head, his eyes slamming shut in the pure blissful agony as she turned around in a sixty-nine, her mouth settling on him. Everything shattered then. The room. His heart. His body.

Cool and sweet, her lips slipped over the tip of him like wet velvet catching fire, then burned down his shaft, clearly intending to take in all of him. Inch by inch, she sent shocking delight through his system.

His mouth found her again. He could barely hold back his own release as her silken thighs wrapped around his head, but he wanted her to come with him. Both of them. Together. At exactly the same time. Just like in the old days. His tongue quickened, his mouth drank her in, his hands smoothed over the gorgeous curve of her backside.

Then everything went black. But he was still waiting. One more second. She was right there. Hovering on the brink while every hot flick of her tongue was making him...

"Please," he gasped, hating that it was he, not she, who'd been reduced to begging. She took it as a command, and as he felt her orgasm, his own came. It swept him off the bed, into the outside air. Into the early morning. Into some heavenly place he'd never visited before this moment. Damn if her tongue hadn't emptied him of every last drop of pleasure he could ever feel.

And then he heard her teasing whisper. "Kick it up another notch."

"Bam," he whispered back.

THE SOUND OF A DOOR jolted Carla awake. Her eyes flew to the clock. It was 9:00 a.m.! A number of things registered at once: first, she'd spent all night, not to mention all morning making love to Tobias who was still lying in bed next to her, snoring. Second, they'd missed breakfast and her stomach was growling. She was starved. And third, a man she'd never seen before was standing there, watching her. Frowning groggily, she could have sworn Tobias had locked the door last night.

She squinted. The man, whoever he was, was good-looking in a Mick Jagger, pretty-boy kind of way. Tall, thin and gaunt. The thick mass of silver hair he wore thrust back from his forehead made him look far too intense for Carla's taste, however. She preferred guys like Tobias who were more down-to-earth and who had a sense of humor. This one was definitely angry.

"Mr. Sloane."

Tobias's rusty voice sounded next to her, sending a

ripple of awareness through her system, along with a memory of what had so recently transpired—at least until his words registered.

"Mr. Sloane?" she echoed, her own voice sounding just as husky as Tobias's. "Oh, no."

Suddenly, Tobias sat up. Only when the covers were whisked over her naked body did she realize that she'd been exposed. Even worse, Tobias overestimated, and for the briefest instant, before Carla could bat away the sheet, her face was covered. Not that she minded. Given the look on Mr. Sloane's, she'd just as soon hide. Or become invisible.

And yet, they'd done nothing wrong. She'd almost married Tobias in the past, after all. And anyway, women could enjoy their sexuality any way they pleased, right?

At least she thought so until she surveyed Sloane Junior again. He looked appalled. His blue eyes were piercing through Tobias who'd gotten out of bed with a grim expression and was quickly pulling on his pants. "Please." Tobias raised a staying hand after jerking up his zipper. "I know what you're thinking, Mr. Sloane, but..."

Sloane Junior's jaw was slack, and Carla suddenly realized that despite his gaunt, dissipated party-boy look, the man was wearing a conservative navy suit with a red-white-and-blue tie. Not a good sign, she decided. The attire definitely fit with what Tobias had told her about Sloane Junior's turning forty and deciding to become more respectable. Despite the adventures he'd had before his last birthday, Sloane Junior was not going to cut her and Tobias any slack.

He said, "You slept with a patient?"

Carla hated it when people spoke about her as if she wasn't there, but she decided, for Tobias's sake, not to say anything.

Tobias was snagging his shirt from the floor. "It's not what it looks like."

But of course, it was exactly what it looked like.

It had felt as good as it looked, too. "We almost got married," she suddenly said now, hoping to help Tobias. "I mean," she clarified, "it's not as if we didn't know each other. I'm not really a patient...not in the usual sense."

Sloane Junior, for all his newfound morals, didn't even do her the courtesy of acknowledging her existence. "We wondered where you were this morning during breakfast," he said to Tobias. "All last night, of course, I was aware you were elsewhere in the building, taking care of staffing problems. I spoke to Dr. MacGregor, who was monitoring this woman's sleep. But now..."

Carla's eyes shot to Tobias. In the brief instant their eyes locked and held, she realized the truth and gasped. "Last night, we didn't—" Her mind raced to the dreams she'd had before this morning, when Tobias had gotten into bed with her, and now they seemed like exactly that—dreams.

When he'd realized she'd had another erotic dream, he'd taken full advantage! Shutting her eyes, she could scarcely believe any of this was happening. Surely, she should be furious at Tobias. But sex with him had been deliciously good. No wonder the door hadn't been locked! And no wonder he'd hedged on the condom question! She sighed. Now she was trapped naked under the covers while two men stared each other down like bucks about to lock horns. It was definitely the wrong time to realize that Tobias had climbed into bed with her when she'd thought it was...what had she called it? A repeat performance. Right.

And yes...given the well-loved feel of her body, not to mention Tobias's previously nude state, that was no dream. Blinking again, she concentrated on her body feelings. Something definitely happened. Now she remembered a little more. The sixty-nine thing. The thing that suddenly made her shudder despite the fact that a very angry Sloane Junior was still in the room.

Tobias's lips had slackened. He didn't take kindly to people telling him how to conduct himself, but he was in an awkward position. "Really," he said. "This is my..." Pausing, he looked very undecided, then he finally said, "uh...my fiancée, Carla DiDolche."

Something wrenched inside her chest, hurting. She'd hardly expected the feeling, but suddenly, she really wished she hadn't come to the clinic. She'd never forgive her mother for still caring about Tobias and trying to play matchmaker. No, with so many unresolved feelings between her and Tobias, Carla definitely didn't want to spend time playing fake fiancée.

"She was having some bad dreams," Tobias continued. "And so I asked her to stay for a couple of nights."

Sloane Junior didn't look convinced, especially not when his eyes leaped to the hand fisted around the sheet she held to her chest. There was no way Carla could hide her bare ring finger without dropping the sheet and exposing an even barer chest, something she wasn't about to do. "Really," she said, nodding, doing her best to sound dignified, which was difficult when you were naked. She wasn't inclined to lie for Tobias, either, she decided, not when he'd lied to her this morning about their having previously made love. Nevertheless, she hated to see him in a jam. "We've known each other a very long time."

Sloane Junior still didn't so much as glance her way.

"May I see you downstairs?" he asked Tobias pointedly.

"Of course."

Sloane Junior turned, as if to go back through the doorway, but then stopped and said, "I believe this makes things decisive, Dr. Free. From what I've seen this morning, I'd be negligent if I withheld the lease on this building from the Preservation Society. My great-great grandfather, Cornelius Sloane, would never condone such behavior."

Carla was tempted to point out that Cornelius Sloane was probably a dirty old man who had lived for his porn collection.

"It's unfair to let this influence your decision," Tobias said reasonably.

Sloane Junior slid a hand down the front of his suit jacket as if feeling each gold, nautically inspired gold button gave him renewed confidence. "I also looked over your research last night. Ms. DiDolche's results throw your theories out of the water."

"Now, wait a minute," began Tobias.

But Sloane Junior held up a hand, palm out. "According to one of your own colleagues, if your guided imagery technique worked, Ms. DiDolche would not have had erotic dreams about her doctor. She'd have had the same recurrent nightmares, but with small changes…"

"I don't know why she didn't." Tobias blew out a frustrated breath. "But it can be explained. If we could just have another chance to—"

"I'm sorry. My decision is final. While you finish dressing, I'll be in the office waiting." Turning on his heel, Sloane Junior prepared to head downstairs again. "We'll proceed directly to an agreement about when you can vacate."

Tobias stared at Sloane Junior's retreating back, then shifted his gaze to Carla. Somehow, Carla wished he hadn't. When she registered his expression, she said, "Now wait a minute. This isn't my fault." In fact, it was she who'd been wronged. It was slowly sinking in that, at least until this morning, all the sex she'd had with Tobias was in her head.

A full unbroken moment passed during which he seemed to be deciding what to say. It was the wrong time to note how sexy he looked when he was mad, with his lips pursed, and his usually dreamy-looking brown eyes narrowed, the irises darker and glinting the way they did when he was in the throes of passion.

"Damn," he suddenly muttered.

She waited for whatever was about to follow. But he simply headed for the door, slipping into his shoes and buttoning his shirt as he moved. And then he followed Sloane Junior downstairs without looking back.

6

WHEN HE FELT her presence behind him, Tobias's frown deepened. He'd been brooding, staring at the old daguerreotype photographs on the walls, his eyes unseeing. As he took a deep breath and forced himself to turn around, focusing his attention where Carla was framed in the doorway of the formal dining room, he silently cursed himself for coming down here where he could be found so easily by her. He would have gone elsewhere, but moments ago, Margaret Craig, who'd spread Sloane Senior's porn collection on the dining table, had called Tobias inside the room so she could gloat over getting the lease. Even worse, she'd quickly excused herself, saying she needed to go to the little girls' room, leaving Tobias to safeguard the pictures, something he'd politely agreed to do simply because his pride wouldn't let him show Margaret—or any other Preservation Society member—his fury. The little girls' room, he thought now, chewing the inside of his cheek. Yeah, right. Sandy Craig had been a late baby, and her mother was pushing seventy.

With a frustrated sigh, he glared at Carla, thrusting his fingers through his hair, lifting the blond strands as he pushed them from his face. Was his dream clinic really going to close? Could his life's work truly go down the tubes? His nearly ten years in college? He couldn't believe it. Nor could he imagine relocating to work in another city. He'd made a home in the Burgh, never meaning to leave. His family was here. He'd bought a house. A little voice played under his thoughts, and before he could push it away, he heard: Carla's here, too.

"Carla," he finally said, his voice dry, terse and communicating his mood perfectly. Right now, she was the only person he wanted to see less than Margaret Craig and Sloane Junior; it hardly mattered that she'd so recently sent him skyrocketing into sensual oblivion. Or actually, it did. Wasn't that why he wanted her gone ASAP? So he wouldn't be confronted by his own male weakness?

She'd gauged his mood, and now her shoulders stiffened. "Tobias."

Too bad she looked even better in her street attire than the pajamas she'd worn last night. A pair of green jeans hugged her hips, molded curving thighs, then flared from the knee into bell bottoms that stylishly skimmed platform sandals. Her legs weren't particularly long, not really, but in those pants they looked like they went all the way up to her armpits. Her toenails, like her T-shirt, were bright red. She said, "Well, aren't you going to say anything?"

"I'm thinking." Just looking at her was more than he could bear right now. Especially since Sloane Junior had just made him sign a paper saying he'd vacate within a matter of months. How was he supposed to get all this equipment out of the building in that time? Much less try to find another clinic space, in the hopes of starting over with the other employees?

He registered Carla's studiously neutral expression,

then he let his gaze drift slowly, pointedly down her long arm until it settled on a hand which was gripped around the strap of her duffel. He didn't move from his position near the old photographs, only lifted an eyebrow. "Leaving so soon?"

"Maybe I'd better."

Ah. So, she'd brought down the duffel expecting him to beg her to stay. Fat chance. She'd broken his heart seven years ago, and now she'd ruined his professional life. Inhaling sharply, he tried not to think of all the years he'd spent in school and the long hours he'd dedicated to the clinic. "They probably miss you at the café," he agreed, keeping his tone just as neutral as her expression. "And Sloane Junior's right. I don't know why the guided dream imagery didn't work on you in the usual way."

"You don't think we should try again?"

For a second, he was sure she was talking about their relationship, not the dream work. As if a quick roll in the hay would change things, he thought, feeling his internal temperature rise. He'd tried to ignore the hopeful note in her voice, and how the air in the room seemed to grow unbearably still. Under other circumstances, he'd have been glad she wasn't mad about his making love to her under the false pretense that they'd done so before. Now, he just wanted her off the premises. Didn't she understand she'd just wrecked his life?

As the moment continued ticking by, he became conscious of the summer sunlight streaming through a window and the chirp of birds outside in the trees, then of his own disheveled state. His clothes were rumpled from being on the floor last night, and although he'd finger-combed his hair on the way downstairs to talk to Sloane Junior, he knew it was a mess. He desperately needed a shower, too.

"Try again?" he finally echoed. "Uh...no." Pausing, he shoved his hands deeply into his jeans pockets and added, "Who knows if we'll even have a clinic?"

Her tone turned acerbic and she all but rolled her eyes. "I'm sure the clinic will still be here tonight, Tobias," she said, her tone implying that he was being ridiculous. Probably, he was.

He offered a shrug. "You never know."

Lips he'd kissed brazenly just hours ago pursed together, forming a tight line. "This isn't my fault," she reminded him flatly, her dark Italian eyes flashing. The quick glint of passion, which he recognized from bed, took his breath.

As she walked inside the room, the belled hems of her pants made a swishing sound. A soft click followed as she shut a heavy carved wooden door, the movement noticeably gentle and exaggerated as if she were desperately trying to control her temper. He registered a thud as she lowered the duffel to the hardwood floor, then he fought the nagging urge to move closer, hating the traitorous desire to feel her body against his and to inhale her scent.

She came toward him, stopping near the dining table. "Really," she began, splaying a hand on the polished surface of the wood, "this isn't my fault, Tobias. Sloane Junior just walked in on us, and..."

Before he could stop himself, Tobias drew his hands out of his jeans pockets and gave in to the impulse to stride forward, coming to a halt when he reached the table. "Not your fault?" he echoed, surprised at the surge of venom in his voice, then even more surprised by the insistent, almost compulsive need to reach out and haul her against his chest. He imagined delivering a harsh, punishing kiss—as if any such assault could teach Carla DiDolche anything.

"Absolutely not my fault," she clarified.

Her tone further tweaked his temper. It was so damn prissy and prim, so devoid of recognition of what she'd done. It was just like the tone she'd used when he'd first tried to ask her why she'd run back down the aisle. Oh, yes, his fingers itched to reach for that long, smooth bare arm and yank her close. Uncomfortably close. The words were out before he could stop them, his voice almost a growl. "Why'd you come here, Carla?" She'd known she wasn't wanted, that it would be hard for both of them.

Her dark eyes widened, her rose-and-cream complexion turning as dusky as twilight. "Because my mother said she'd come back and run the café if I didn't."

"Really?" He was starting to believe she must have come here intentionally to seduce him. How else could he have wound up in bed with a woman he usually avoided like the plague? But then maybe Mary DiDolche was matchmaking. After all, she'd loved him like the son she'd never had, just as his mother had accepted Carla like an only daughter.

"Uh-huh," said Carla, nodding her head in a way that made her curls bounce—and made him long to touch them. "She threatened me."

"So, you're afraid she'll come back and take over the café?"

She nodded again. "She thinks the dreams get in the way of my running the place effectively."

"I see."

"And...I came to have you cure me." She sucked in a quick breath. "Which you didn't."

As if he was incompetent. "And I guess that's your rationale for closing my clinic?" he returned, his deceptively calm voice masking the inner turmoil that was starting to churn inside him. Dammit, he felt as if someone had inserted a handle with a crank into his side, and now they were turning the crank for all it was worth. He sure wished they'd stop.

Her lips parted. "Tobias, I didn't lose the lease. Sloane Junior just walked in on us and—"

He cut her off, saying, "Sure you did. Just like you broke my heart seven years ago, Carla. Every time you walk into my life, I lose something else—"

Her gasp stopped him, and the expression in eyes that looked round and owlish now turned serious and even forbidding, as if she dared him to say one more word. "You're the one who got into bed with me this morning," she pointed out, tightening her grip around the back of a dining chair, her knuckles turning white, then pink, as if she might rip the delicate carving right off the wood.

He couldn't help but edge closer, halting when they were nose to nose. "You asked me to get into bed with you," he corrected.

Her eyes lasered into his. "I thought we'd slept together already," she returned, her voice careful, the vocal equivalent of lifting a precious glass object. "I thought my dream from last night was real and you know that. You took full advantage."

Ah. So now he was the guilty party. As he gazed into her eyes, his blood really started to boil. For an instant, he was back in the past, at their wedding, his heart hammering with anticipation as her bridesmaids were led down the aisle. He wasn't proud of it, but suddenly, he wanted to hurt Carla. Without her and this clinic, the distasteful truth was that he had nothing left. Unless you counted his house, he supposed. "I only took advantage," he muttered, "because I had fantasies of bringing you to the edge of satisfaction, then walking away."

He wanted her to be very clear on that fact, but it only brought a gleam of challenge to her bewitching eyes. "Guess you weren't able to back off, huh?"

She was right on the money. Wild horses couldn't have dragged him off Carla's hot body. He swallowed hard, his own gaze sliding to the pulse point at her throat, which was flickering like the filament inside a burning light bulb. Heat and excitement seemed to charge the air. "You always were good in bed, Carla," he admitted.

"Good enough that you lied just to have sex with me this morning?"

He begged himself not to, but he rejoined with, "You could at least return a compliment."

Ignoring him, she said, "You lied."

"Not directly."

"By omission."

"Apparently."

Her dark eyes were still fixed intently on his, and they'd turned midnight black, just like the curling hair that skimmed her shoulders. "Good," she muttered, her voice catching huskily, "because you need to understand your part in this, Tobias. You're not going to walk away thinking I cost you your clinic. I know what this place means to you. Sloane Junior caught us in bed for one reason, and one reason only—because you got into the bed.''

She had a point there, loathsome as it was to admit it. ''Maybe,'' he countered, barely aware he'd edged forward, just close enough that the heat seeping from her skin could be registered. His voice lowered a notch, turning angrier even as it became more seductive. ''But the truth remains. Every time you come into my life, Carla, things get ugly.''

That hurt her. As vague, barely discernible emotions passed in her eyes, warring feelings claimed him. No, he really couldn't help it. He wanted to hurt her. ''Ten years,'' he added. ''That's how long I went to school. This place is my life.'' Just as she'd almost been his life once upon a time.

''You had a part in what happened,'' she repeated.

For a second he was tongue-tied. Then he gave in, reached out and curled his fingers around her upper arm. With gentleness he couldn't begin to feel, he drew her toward him, giving a quick shake of his head, a denial of how good she felt. ''Not really,'' he said, gazing down into her face, his eyes riveting on a mouth he'd prefer not to notice.

''Of course you did.''

Why the hell didn't this woman understand? ''Not really,'' he repeated, his voice dropping to a husky whisper as his mouth lowered almost of its own accord, stopping shy of settling on hers. ''How was I supposed to say no?'' he demanded softly, ''when I'd watched you sleep two nights in a row? In that hot, tight little green T-shirt?'' Sucking a breath between his teeth, he added, ''Don't you know what you do to me, Carla?''

She looked positively stunned. Her jaw was unhinged, her lips parted, her eyes like saucers. She sounded shocked, as if she'd just gotten more of a response from him than she'd bargained for. ''I was just saying you didn't really have a right to be mad,'' she managed. ''You climbed into bed with me, Tobias. And...''

As her voice drifted off, he realized his breath had gone shallow. Bands circled around his chest, squeezing the life out of him. Her mouth was so close, just inches away. With near desperation, he tried not to think of where that mouth had been earlier, how those red lips had looked circling the most intimate part of him, and how mind-bendingly good it had felt. He seriously considered dragging her back upstairs, into that empty unmade four-poster with the still-mussed sheets. Suddenly, he didn't give a damn about Sloane Junior or the clinic. For the space of a heartbeat, he knew he'd throw it all away just to have sex with her again. And then he came to his senses. Abruptly, he let go of her arm, nearly thrusting her away. ''You'd better go now, Carla.''

Her chin lifted in surprise, and she looked vaguely confused. No doubt, she was wondering what was happening to him. Hadn't he just said he wanted her? Dammit, he did, but... ''I can't let you ruin my life again.''

Her chin dropped, and she uttered a short, sharp little inhalation, just the sort she made when she got hot and bothered. He hardly expected her next words. "You married Sandy Craig."

Only because Carla had dumped him so publicly. "What's that got to do with anything?"

"You act like I'm the only one who did anything wrong."

"Something was wrong with me marrying Sandy?"

"Well, maybe not, but..."

"I guess I have a right to marry whoever the hell I want," he muttered.

She merely stared at him, her eyes turning as dark as pitch now, making her look like proverbial Italian women in movies, driven by passions beyond their control. "I've never asked," she said, her voice tight, her words succinct, "but I think I'd like to know."

He waited. Whatever it was, she had never asked for one simple reason: they'd never talked. He said, "What?"

There was a long silence during which he could have counted to ten. Once more, he registered her proximity, and the sweet tang of her body's scent. When she spoke, her voice was so low he could barely make out the words. "Did you love her?"

No, he thought, but he considered a long moment, anyway, nearly as long as it had taken her to ask the question, then he said, looking exasperated, "None of your business, Carla."

She didn't look so sure. Her vibrant jet eyes were melting, turning soft and gooey in a way he definitely didn't want to acknowledge. Sex was one thing. What happened this morning, not to mention in Carla's dreams, had been as hot as summer, too. But this talk was getting way too personal for Tobias.

"Fine," she finally said. "It's none of my business."

He tried to tell himself he didn't care as she spun around and headed toward where she'd set down the duffel. Despite the circumstances, his eyes drifted over the squared shoulders that had always bespoken a determination he loved, and the softly curving spine that arched so deliciously when they had sex, to her backside and the legs that looked so damnably long in the green jeans. Sighing audibly, she leaned and curled her fingers around the handle of the duffel. Lifting it, she turned toward him again.

He damned her for taking his breath away. Was Carla DiDolche really about to walk out of his life for good? Had she really asked him if he'd loved Sandy Craig? Did she really care? Did she wished she hadn't run back down that aisle? His heart lurched, but he offered no telltale outward sign that his internal life had gone haywire.

Her back was so ramrod straight that she could have been lying on an ironing board. "I guess this is goodbye, Tobias."

The moment seemed to hang suspended in space, like a pendulum that wasn't quite ready to swing back in the other direction. Was this really the last word he was going to say to Carla DiDolche? "Yeah," he managed to say with a quick nod. "I guess this is goodbye."

Just as the words were out, she gasped. He realized her eyes had slid to the artwork Margaret Craig had left scattered across the dining table. "I can't believe it!" Carla breathlessly exclaimed, saying the very last thing he expected. "It's the golden underwear!"

HER FINGERS UNCURLED from around the duffel strap and as the bag hit the floor, she lurched forward, heading toward the dining table again, unable to believe her eyes. Staring in shock, she took in what she could see of a watercolor. Carefully, mindful of the artwork's delicacy, she edged the picture from under the others and held it up to the light.

Her lips parted in astonishment. Yes, she hadn't been mistaken! She'd know this item anywhere. The golden underwear she'd seen in her dreams was exactly the same as in the picture. But it wasn't really a pair of underwear, after all. It was a medieval chastity belt, viewed from the back. As her gaze dropped over the metal waistband, then the metal-plated inner divider piece that formed the leg holes, she wondered what the front had looked like. In the bottom right-hand corner, the artist had painted the words, "breeches of Florentine gold, probably from 1400 A.D."

"Unbelievable," she whispered, barely aware that Tobias had sidled behind her.

"It's a chastity belt," he said.

"A chastity belt," she repeated. Of course! She should have known. But when she'd first seen it in her nightmares, she hadn't yet entered grade school. So, she'd simply referred to the item as golden underwear. If she didn't feel so confused, she'd laugh. "A chastity belt," she murmured again. What was going on? How was this possible? Turning, she glanced over her shoulder at Tobias. As she gazed into his eyes, her cheek almost grazed his, and her heart fluttered at the near contact. A swift recollection of what they'd done a few hours ago flitted into her mind. She remembered his taste and how crazy he'd driven her with lust. "This is what I saw in my dreams," she said.

He squinted as if he, too, was recalling their tryst in the four poster bed. "Huh?"

Obviously, he still didn't get it. "My dreams," she repeated. "You know...I always say the man lifts a pair of golden underwear? Well." She lifted the picture. "This is them."

He peered at her in disbelief. "You're sure?"

She nodded quickly, her heart racing. "An exact replica."

"But how..."

She shrugged. As far back as she could remember, she'd been haunted by her dreams. Even now, as she thought about them, her fear became palpable. Her throat tightened; her mouth turned mealy. Adrenaline rushed into her system. Suddenly, she was trapped in the mysterious stairwell again; the mazelike steps went upward, downward, and even sideways. Nothing seemed to make any logical sense. And then the image was replaced by the room she'd dreamed of.... Darkness faded into the musty corners and a man was lifting the golden underwear with his beefy fingers.

Something swift and visceral locked around her, leaving a bone-chill, as if an icy ghostly finger had just touched her soul. Then she heard the man's rusty voice saying, "If you marry, you will die."

Her heart hammering, Carla realized that her fingers were trembling. Quickly, she glided the picture back onto the polished surface of the table, as if she could no longer stand to touch it, just as Tobias's voice sounded right next to her ear.

"You're sure?" he asked again.

"Yeah."

She turned toward him again in the limited space. Despite his anger and their previously charged exchange, or maybe because of it, she felt her body thrum with excitement. Tension had her wound up like a kid's top. "Don't you see?" she murmured. "It's not a dream. Not a nightmare. It's real."

His gaze shot past her to the picture. "The watercolor isn't very detailed," he mused.

"Maybe not, but I'd recognize this chastity belt anywhere," she countered. "Really. It's what I've always called the golden underwear," she insisted, taking in the contours of the golden belt. "And it's distinctive. I must have seen it from the back, the way it's shown here. I've no idea what the front looks like."

Tobias shook his head. "But that's crazy."

Her heart missed a beat. He had to believe her. "I'm not making this up," she persisted. "The chastity belt in this picture is exactly what I've seen in my nightmares."

"I'm not saying you're mistaken. I just…"

She knew he hated her. He wanted her to leave. He'd made that clear, but this was her one chance to redeem herself. She didn't want him to lose the clinic. "Tobias," she urged. "I know it sounds nuts, but the chastity belt in this picture is what I've seen in my dreams, and there's got to be some reasonable explanation."

She could still barely believe what she was seeing, even though the picture was before her eyes. What connection could Cornelius Sloane's porn collection have to the nightmares she'd endured her whole life?

Would whatever she might uncover mean that her nightmares would finally end?

"I guess this could be a Jungian event," Tobias murmured.

"Jungian?"

"Carl Jung," he clarified. "A psychologist. Author of *Dreams and the Unconscious.* According to him, all of us have similar images buried in our unconscious minds. It's possible that you and the artist both had access to the same image through what Jung called the collective unconscious."

She could barely follow what he was saying. It was too difficult when his chest brushed hers ever so lightly, and when she was so confused about the argument they'd just had. One minute, she'd been grabbing the duffel and heading out the door. And now...

"You're thinking that the chastity belt isn't real?" she managed to ask. "Just a figment of my imagination?"

"Maybe. Possibly, you and this artist imagined the same thing." He looked indecisive. Also, he looked as if this sudden attention to his work, which was the passion of his life, had temporarily erased the anger he'd expressed toward Carla just moments before. Her mind was still reeling. Had she really asked Tobias if he'd loved Sandy Craig? What had come over her? Of course he'd loved Sandy; he'd married her.

He was chewing his lip. "Maybe..."

Before he could finish, she shook her head, acting on her own gut instinct. "Tobias," she said, "I think it's real. I think I saw this chastity belt before."

"What makes it feel real?"

Sighing, she shook her head. "I don't know. Just a feeling."

He nodded. "Where did you see it?"

She stared at the picture on the table again, wracking her brain. After a long moment, she shook her head again. "I don't know. My sixth sense says I did, though. As far as I know, I only saw it when I was in that dark, dank room…where the man lifted it to the light."

"It's possible that the chastity belt's real," he finally conceded. "And that would explain why you didn't respond to the electrical impulses we administered in the way we expected."

She tried to tamp down the wave of excitement. That her nightmares might end was too much to hope. Suddenly, her excitement morphed into a shudder. What if she came face to face with the villain in her nightmare? Once more, she heard the gruff voice say, "If you marry, you will die." "If the belt's real," she murmured, her voice catching, "then that means the man is real."

Tobias's eyes narrowed in concern. "That's the logical conclusion. But let's not jump to it. Think hard. Try to remember, Carla. Where—outside your dreams—might you have seen a chastity belt…"

"Maybe in a museum somewhere."

"We can ask someone in the Society," Tobias said, his curiosity overtaking his feelings toward the group.

She shut her eyes for a long moment, then opened them. "Nothing," she muttered. "As far as I know, I've never seen the belt or the man, not really. But it feels so real. And the picture's right here…."

"Maybe you repressed a memory," Tobias suggested.

Her eyes slid to the picture. Staring at it, she half

expected it to vanish. Truly, this seemed so impossible. Did this watercolor hold the key to an event that had haunted her since childhood? An event that had kept her from marrying Tobias Free?

"What could my dreams have to do with Cornelius Sloane?" she murmured. Considering further, she shook her head. "Honestly," she admitted, barely able to believe she was still standing here with Tobias any more than she'd just found a clue to the mysterious golden underwear. "I never really believed in repressed memories. I like to read about them in novels, of course. They can make for a good mystery, but do you really think you can forget things that happen?"

"Minds can be tricky."

So could feelings, not that Carla was about to mention it at the moment. "I guess you're right, Tobias."

"You thought we'd slept together," he reminded.

Kinetic sparks suddenly ricocheted between them. She realized she was gazing into his eyes as if mesmerized. She couldn't help but say, "We did sleep together."

They both sucked in breaths.

Then swallowed.

Then looked away.

And then they looked into each other's eyes again.

"Look," she said quickly. "I really can't come up with a reasonable explanation as to why an image from my dreams would be in this drawing." How could something from inside her own mind be in a nineteenth century steel baron's porn collection? "But if what I saw is real, not a dream, then that does explain why your guided dream imagery didn't work in the way you expected, and..."

Was it her imagination, or had Tobias's eyes glued to her mouth as if he had no other thought except kissing her? "And?" Why, when the man used simple words such as the conjunction "and" did it sound like he was whispering sweet nothings? She shrugged with a casualness she couldn't begin to feel. She wanted one more night with Tobias. Even if they didn't sleep together, she wanted him near as she drifted off to sleep. Yes, she didn't want to leave the clinic. She knew that now. She'd missed Tobias like the devil. "And I think I should stay one more night," she said, finding her voice.

"I'm not a researcher anymore," he reminded her, his voice unreadable as he referred to the loss of the building to the Preservation Society.

Before she thought it through, Carla reached out and curled her fingers around his elbow. "But you could be," she urged. "Maybe if you monitor my dreams again, this time operating under the assumption that they're memories, not dreams, something will change."

The lure of the challenge was too much for Tobias. "Sloane Junior will have a fit if you stay another night."

"You lost the lease, anyway," she said, a glint of wickedness in her eyes. "So, who cares?"

Tobias actually smiled. "Good point."

She suppressed a shudder at the thought of curling up in the four-poster where they'd gotten down and dirty this morning. "Maybe I'll really remember something more tonight," she said hopefully. "Maybe I did see this picture in a book or a museum when I was a kid."

"But that wouldn't explain the presence of the man."

She sighed. "True. Unless he was also in a picture I saw."

Tobias shook his head. "The dream's too emotional. It would make better sense if you..."

"Actually saw a man hold up this chastity belt?"

He nodded. "Why not? In fact, that might account for why your dreams so often seem real. Maybe it's your subconscious, trying to point out that what seemed like a dream is really a memory."

Her breath caught. It made so much sense. And yet it seemed incredibly farfetched, too. Nevertheless, she was willing to try anything to stop the nightmares. She wanted another night with Tobias, too—any way she could get it. Maybe, if she was lucky, she could lure him back into bed.

"If you really saw this chastity belt, allowing us to prove this is a memory, not a dream," he murmured, "that would fix the problems Sloane Junior found in my research."

"And if you can do that," Carla urged, "it might be easier to get a new lease somewhere else in the Burgh."

That was enough to convince Tobias. "All right."

Carla was still wishing he was motivated by wanting her, not by wanting to fix his research, when the heavy carved door swung open. She and Tobias turned, and found themselves facing Margaret Craig.

"My, my, my," said the matronly woman. "If it isn't Carla DiDolche."

Carla knew the other woman by sight because Sandy had been a cheerleader and her mother had attended all the football games. "Hello, Mrs. Craig," she said, not liking the woman's tone any more than the fact that her daughter had married Tobias.

Margaret smiled. "Did you hear that the Preservation Society is going to open its gallery?" She flashed Tobias a smile. "Tobias was just congratulating us!"

Carla doubted it. Apparently, when her daughter's marriage to Tobias ended, Margaret had carried a grudge. "Really?" Carla returned pleasantly.

"Oh, yes."

Margaret Craig was definitely gloating. When she nodded in affirmation, Carla felt a knot of loyalty form in the pit of her stomach. No way was she going to let this woman take away Tobias's lease. Somehow, Carla had to put this mess to rights. She wasn't sure how, but she figured she could start by remembering....

7

BLINKING SLEEP FROM HER eyes, Carla glanced at the clock on the mantle as she took off the electrodes and slipped from bed. "Nearly three in the morning," she murmured, turning toward Tobias who was stationed behind the glass partition.

In the faint illumination from a desk lamp, his expression was hard to read, and she felt a tug of annoyance. Oh, she'd definitely understood his anger earlier. After all, he'd just lost the lease, but hadn't their lovemaking affected him? She'd been climbing the walls, her insides going into overdrive, but he looked thoroughly unmoved.

Not to mention gorgeous. As he rose from behind the desk, heat flooded her, and it took real effort to hold back a wistful sigh. Because Sloane Junior had announced his decision, Tobias hadn't bothered to put on the jacket and tie again. Instead, he was wearing the kind of clothes he usually favored: threadbare jeans that hugged his slender hips and a skin-hugging black T-shirt that outlined his pectorals. Behind him, the shadow he cast against a wall loomed nearly to the ceiling, so he looked particularly tall and lean. Her eyes trailed sleepily up the long runner's legs that had jettisoned him to track fame in high school, then to where his jeans lovingly cupped his crotch, fitting as tightly as a hand, and finally over the shirt and to his face again.

In the dim light, his blond hair looked dark, and it was thrust back from a face dancing with shadows. Most strands were separated, probably from his constant finger combing, but some fell into his eyes, making her itch to cross the room and push them back into place. Blowing out another sigh—this one more frustrated—she wished he'd show some sign that he still wanted her.

He said, "You were deep in REM sleep."

Blinking once more, she realized she'd come to a standstill, next to the bed. "Huh?"

"The dream stage," he explained. "What woke you up?"

Wishing you'd climb into bed with me. What they'd done this morning simply wasn't enough. Like a sexual hors d'oeuvre it had only whetted her appetite, leaving her craving more. Yes, it was like eating only half an Italian Hoagie from Tessaro's and then having your mouth water for the rest of the day. Having Tobias love her in a sixty-nine position was great, of course, but now she wanted the whole enchilada, so to speak. "What's with all the food metaphors," she whispered under her breath, a smile tugging at her lips. Whatever it was, her stomach suddenly growled.

"Hungry?" he asked.

Starved. At least for sex. With you. "A little." She glanced up and realized Tobias was watching her cautiously, as if he half feared she might suddenly hop back into bed and rip off all her clothes. If he wasn't careful, she just might. "Uh...I'm not sure what woke me," she added.

"You'd just started the REM phase. You couldn't have been dreaming long."

She squinted at him in the darkness. "I wasn't."

"Looked like the nightmare was starting to come back."

For the first time in her life, Carla almost wished it had. Even that terror would be better than the erotic, edgy dreams that had otherwise claimed her consciousness. They, like the sex this morning, had done nothing but drive her crazy with longing. Especially since Tobias had been avoiding her all day, treating her like a lowly private on a ship where everyone had Legionnaire's disease.

"Uh...yeah," she finally said, groggily reaching for the white terry-cloth bathrobe she'd left at the foot of the bed. "I was in that weird staircase again."

As she drew the robe around herself, she felt her cheeks warming. Nope...now there was no mistaking the hunger in the flicker of Tobias's gaze. Her pink silk shorts and camisole were more suggestively feminine than the green pajamas she'd been wearing for the past two nights, not that she'd expected to wear these at all. By now, she'd thought she'd be home. She slipped into house slippers, then headed for the partition. Just as she reached Tobias, her sleep-fogged mind seemed to clear. "That's it," she muttered throatily. "That's why I woke up."

The lazy way he lifted an eyebrow and surveyed her from under heavily lidded eyes made her heart flutter. "Why?"

She squinted. "C'mon," she said in a non sequitor, reaching to curl her hand around his elbow, then wishing she hadn't when she felt his impossibly smooth skin gliding under her fingertips. He drew back, barely perceptibly. "Where?"

She couldn't help but chuckle. "What?" she teased. "Did you think I got up to try to drag you into bed, Dr. Free?"

Before he could stop himself, he smiled, just a quick upcurl of his lip and the flash of straight white teeth in the dark. His eyes settled on hers, the sparkle in the irises taking some of the sting out of his words. "Try being the operative word."

Her throat tightened. Yes, he was definitely sorry he'd given in to temptation. Making a point of ignoring his response, she shifted the subject. "Actually, I want to go downstairs," she said airily, tightening her fingers under his elbow and guiding him from the room.

"Downstairs?" he asked as they reached the door.

"Yeah." She nodded, squinting into the dim hallway, trying to get her bearings as images from her dreams flitted into her consciousness. Everything had turned as impenetrably black as a starless night, so dark that for a moment she hadn't known if her eyes were open or shut. Was she sleeping? Or had she been awake? Unsure, she darted her eyes in the pitch darkness, but still, she saw nothing. Which way should she run? Was anybody else here?

"Hello?" she'd whispered, fighting down her rising terror.

No answer had come, so she'd taken a shaky step and realized she was walking downstairs. Had she been dreaming? Or sleepwalking? She'd felt as if she was going out of her mind. Panic assaulted her. Her heart thudded. She was all alone. How would she get home now? "Mama?" she'd whispered. "Papa?" Her throat had tightened, closing like a trap. She couldn't even smell coffee from the café! Her hand found a wall, and she'd run her trembling fingers along the plaster but found no light switch. Where was she?

Tobias's voice sounded in a near whisper. "Why are we going downstairs? A refrigerator raid?"

She blinked against the dim light as they stepped onto the red-carpeted staircase. "No," she whispered back, keeping her voice low, so as not to wake any of the patients. "Although, now that you mention it, I could use some of that chocolate mousse and whipped cream they served for dessert."

"That can probably be arranged."

She just wished he'd be licking it off choice parts of her anatomy. "I take it you have an in with the establishment?" she teased, sleepily stifling a yawn.

His tone was gruff. "I used to."

She could have kicked herself. "Sorry," she murmured, wishing she hadn't made him think about the lease.

A brief uncomfortable silence fell as they continued going downstairs, and she tried to avert her attention from him to her surroundings—taking in the red runner on the steps, the dark oil paintings hung near the landing, an oil lamp on a table in the front foyer. But it was no use. Tobias was jostling her side, sending sparks of awareness through her system, and although she didn't think he was doing it intentionally, she was getting aroused. Very aroused, in fact. Another wave of wistful sadness twisted inside her. Why couldn't he feel how perfectly they fit together? And how warm their brushing bodies were? It would be so simple to turn toward each other on the stairs, embrace and share a deep, hot kiss...

When his husky whisper sounded, an unanticipated shiver went down her spine that had nothing to do with her nightmares. "Now where?"

Oh, she had plenty of ideas, not that he'd go for any of them. What about bed, she thought. "The dining room," she said aloud, heading that way. "I want to see the picture of my apartment again."

"Your apartment?" he echoed as they entered a long, dark hallway.

She nodded. "Yeah." Her mind drifted to her dreams again. Something was niggling at her consciousness; it was like a slow annoying tickle. Or a word that was right on the tip of her tongue. "Like I was saying, I had the dream where I'm stuck on the stairs again..."

"The ones that go up, down and sideways?"

"Yeah. And there were changes in the dream, too."

"Changes?"

Experiencing another shiver, she instinctively reached for Tobias. Surprisingly, he let her settle against him as they continued walking, and he rested his fingers lightly on her shoulder, coming close enough that his chest grazed her back. It wasn't a sensual gesture, unfortunately, but a manly, protective move, not that Carla was going to complain. Don't look a gift horse in the mouth, she thought, nestling nearer and feeling pleased when his fingers flexed on her skin.

"Changes?" he prodded again as they entered the dining room. "In the dream?"

She nodded. As she described them, she hugged her

robe more tightly around herself. Even in daylight, the mansion was huge, cavernous and foreboding; as Tobias had pointed out when she'd arrived, it looked like something out of a Stephen King novel. But at night, in Carla's view, the place got downright creepy. As her eyes darted toward into nooks and crannies, she tried to ignore all the creaking sounds that defied explanation.

When she was finished describing her dream, she added, "Maybe it's not a dream at all, Tobias. Maybe it really is a memory, just like you thought. Either way, for some reason, I remembered more than usual." Before tonight, she'd never talked in the dream, nor had she ever searched for a light switch.

From somewhere far off, a floor board creaked, and she shuddered. "I hope there aren't any ghosts down here."

"Boo," whispered Tobias.

She sent him a droll look. "Sorry." She hesitated, but couldn't stop herself from saying, "You're much too male."

"Ghosts can be male."

"Alive and male."

The conversation ended when Tobias flicked on a squat lamp that sat on a marble topped table, then noticed her concerned expression. "What?"

She shrugged, and as her eyes adjusted to the dim light of the room, she tried to suppress another shudder. "I don't know," she said, unsure of whether the creepy mansion or her dream was causing the emotional unrest.

Tobias came to her side again, this time surprising her by ghosting a hand around her waist to guide her toward the old photographs on the wall. "Scared?" he murmured as if he'd registered the wave of prickles wending down her spine.

"Sort of," she admitted.

"You should be. Sloane Junior might catch you down here in your pajamas."

She crinkled her nose. "It would serve him right."

"True."

"This place is straight out of Frankenstein movies," she added. "And my dreams are always so disturbing. I really wish they'd stop..." They'd been such an albatross around her neck, and she'd give anything to live without the threat of them. Suddenly, she yelped, jumping away from Tobias. Only after she'd done so did she realize he'd playfully pinched her just to scare her.

"You move fast," he teased.

"You louse!" She spun to face him. As she swatted him, he quickly grabbed her hand, then closed his over her fist. Her breath stilled. Everything inside her went haywire. Heat flashed like white lightning through her body, catching on nerves before zipping along sinews. Suddenly, her pulse was pounding too hard, and when her breath came again, it was far too shallow. She had a fantasy of them doing it—right here, right now—on the long, formal nineteenth-century table. The hand cupping hers was so huge...so perfect and dark from the summer sun. Hers was completely enveloped in it, and nothing more than the pressure of the long fingers nearly touching her wrist was maddening. How could such an innocent touch make her heart hammer? Her knees go weak? Make her damp with longing?

She inhaled sharply when he let go.

Disappointment curled inside her, but it didn't last long. Before he turned away to focus his attention on the old photographs, she saw the smoky heat in his eyes. No matter how much he hated her for the past, he wanted her right now, and the realization sent relief through her. No matter how long they'd been apart, Tobias Free would never stop craving her. She was inside him, a part of him. Strumming through his blood. Dancing in his veins. Even though he'd married Sandy Craig, what they'd shared together would never be forgotten. It would live on forever....

Somehow, it seemed like just the right kind of revelation to have in such a ghostly old mansion. Carla's breath ceased for a heartbeat, and her eyes stung, blurring with tears that she blinked back. If he noticed and asked why she was crying, she truly wouldn't know how to put her feelings into words, but for a second, her relationship with Tobias seemed to be the most important thing in her life again. Maybe it always had been.

And he was so oblivious. What a typical male! He was simply standing there with his hands shoved deeply into the pockets of his threadbare blue jeans...hands that had touched her in all her secret places...jeans that she longed to reach out and touch, herself. Sucking in a breath, she tried not to imagine how the fabric would feel. It was worn to the fine, watery texture of silk, and she'd like nothing more to run the flat of her palm between his legs and then upward, over the firm male bulge. She wanted to see him shudder again and throw his head back in ecstacy as she slowly caressed him. She wanted to relive every second of their glory days....

Those stupid tears pushed at her eyelids again, and she inwardly cursed herself for getting so weepy and being so damnably, ridiculously sentimental. Face it, she thought. She was never going to have this man again, sexually or otherwise. In fact, he'd done exactly what he'd said he'd wanted to: gotten her hot and bothered and then walked away, just to drive her crazy.

She guessed she deserved it. After all, she'd behaved in a way that had never fully made sense to her. That, in itself, was scary. Shouldn't a woman know her own mind? What were the deep, dark secrets that lay underneath her nightmares? Taking a deep breath, she inched closer to Tobias, determined to ignore everything about him, from the heat seeping from his body, to his masculine scent, to the way he suddenly turned to look at her, making her feel as if she was the only woman in the world.

"You okay?" he asked, peering into her eyes.

"Uh...yeah."

It's over between us, she tried to remind herself as she stared up into those melting dark, dreamy eyes that made everything inside her start running like a river with a fast current. No, the way Tobias Free looked at women was nothing personal at all. No doubt, every woman experienced this exact feeling: that his eyes said he could make them climax with nothing more than a glance.

"So?" he said. "What about it?"

She was still staring at him. "Huh?" She truly couldn't say anything more intelligent than that.

He squinted. "The picture," he reminded her. "Why did you want to see it?"

"Oh, right," she managed to say.

Turning her attention to the wall, she took in the old, sepia-toned photograph again. The street in front of DiDolche's and Gato and Gambolini's was busy with what looked to be early morning crowds, and smoke from Sloane's steel mills rolled across the sky as businessmen in old-fashioned waistcoats jaywalked, threading their way around horses and buggies.

"I don't know," she murmured. "All I know is that when I woke up, I was thinking about this picture. And my first night here—" She paused, thinking back. "I was visualizing it before my nightmare began." She continued staring at the picture, letting it transport her to another time in history.

"Looks like they were almost finished building it," Tobias commented.

She nodded. "It's interesting to see a picture of your home that was taken over a hundred years ago."

"It's pretty unusual," he agreed, chuckling softly in appreciation. "It hasn't changed much, either."

Carla shook her head. "Hardly at all." Even today, the same green, gold-tipped letters spelled out the DiDolche name on the plate glass. A smile curled her lips as she visualized the marble tiles, old tables and tin ceiling.

"The bench is still out there."

"Grandpapa Sal replaced it."

"It looks exactly the same."

"He had it made to match a picture we have at home."

"Nothing like tradition."

"It's nice to feel like you're a part of history."

As he jostled her side, she felt almost sorry she'd

said the words since it only served as a reminder of their own personal past. "Seeing as we're all living," he said, clearly trying to make light of the moment, "it would be hard not to be part of history."

She playfully elbowed him. "How philosophical."

"They don't call me Doctor Free for nothing."

"Better than the kind of doctor you have to pay for, seeing how expensive doctors can be."

He guffawed. "DiDolche," he said. "You need to go back to bed. Jokes are definitely not your thing at three in the morning."

Once more, she wished he was coming back to bed with her. Ignoring the thought, she laughed softly, and something warm and sweet moved through her when she felt his body relax against hers. For just a second, it really felt like the old days, when they'd tease each other and giggle together, like they were still kids instead of young adults. Their eyes met, and she could have sworn he read her mind and shared her thoughts. When he said nothing, she sobered, turning her attention back to the picture. "It's the scaffolding," she murmured after a moment. "That's what I was thinking about when I woke up."

His eyes followed hers, taking in the makeshift staircase that ran the length of the block, from the topmost floor of DiDolche's to the ground floor of Gato and Gambolini's.

"Good," said Tobias. "That must mean that whatever's buried in your subconscious is starting to surface. If it's a dream, not a memory, maybe the electrical impulses really are starting to make changes to your thinking. If it's a memory, then things are simply starting to come back. Any idea why this picture grabbed you?''

Deep in thought, she shrugged. ''Maybe just because it's of my apartment.''

''Maybe,'' he said noncommittally.

''I don't know,'' she added. ''But what if...'' As her voice trailed off, darker images invaded her consciousness. For a moment, the present seemed to vanish and she was lost in time...lost in the dream again, looking around wildly, her eyes wide open and trying to pierce the impenetrable, inky darkness.

''If?''

Glancing up, she realized Tobias was staring at her intently. As she stared back, she registered that just looking at him made it easier for her to gather her thoughts. Somehow, he'd made so many things in her life easier. Suddenly, she remembered how he used to help out her father at the café, acting like the son Larry DiDolche had never had. Tobias had relished the role, and while Carla's father had never faulted her, she knew he'd regretted the loss of his special relationship with Tobias. Probably, Laura Free and her husband, Jack, felt the same way about Carla.

Feeling a rush of guilt, she forced her mind back to the present. ''I don't know,'' she said, shaking her head and feeling unsure. ''But what if there was a similar staircase on the back of the building?''

He caught her drift immediately. ''Was that what you dreamed?''

''Not exactly, but...''

''You're thinking it might still be there? Walled up by the building's exterior?''

She nodded. ''Maybe,'' she returned, her voice suddenly catching with excitement. ''What if...'' Pausing, she free-associated, letting her mind wander.

''Keep talking,'' said Tobias.

''Maybe there's a crawl space that leads to it,'' she guessed. ''I can't really visualize anything, but it seems possible that only the staircase on the building's front was removed. Maybe it was easier just to wall up another one on the back....''

''So there's an access from someplace inside the café?''

''One that leads to a stairway,'' she agreed. ''Most likely, it would be inside my apartment.''

''You're thinking you got trapped inside it when you were a kid?''

Somehow, that sounded exactly right. ''Yeah. I know it sounds weird, though. And I never heard my folks mention the staircase. It seems like they'd know about such a thing.''

Tobias considered. ''Maybe. But the place was built a long time ago.''

Carla could only laugh. ''Oh, c'mon,'' she chided. ''You know my father. He prides himself on cataloguing every piece of DiDolche history.'' Even as she said the words, she tried not to recall the scrapbooks and photo albums he'd bought before the wedding.

''That he does,'' said Tobias, his tone cryptic. After a moment, he laughed softly, as if with fond memories of her father, and the sound went through her bloodstream like dominoes falling down. She could barely believe she was really standing here with him—laughing and talking. ''Yeah,'' he said softly. ''Larry wouldn't take too kindly to knowing we thought he was a poor historian.''

Her words were low, barely audible. ''He misses you.'' A moment passed, making her sorry she'd said it.

Tobias drew a deep breath. ''Yeah. Me, too.''

Now she wasn't so sorry. When he offered nothing more, she murmured, ''I wonder if I'm right? Maybe I stumbled onto those stairs when I was sleepwalking.''

Tobias loosed a low wolf whistle, seemingly mostly in relief since the conversation had turned away from their families. ''Wouldn't that be incredible? Maybe, after all these years, your nightmares are about to start making sense to you.''

''That seems too good to be true.'' Just like being here with him. Inside her chest, her heart seemed to swell until she thought it might stretch to breaking. She didn't want to project too much, to think about what that could mean...for them. And yet she suddenly heard the rusty voice that had haunted her for years saying, ''If you marry, you will die.'' If she understood whatever plagued her more fully would she be free to love? Would it matter?

She hazarded a glance at Tobias, blowing out a long, heartfelt sigh as she took in his tight jeans and clingy T-shirt. He looked like a *Playgirl* centerfold. Or he would, if his jeans fly was unzipped just enough to show an enticing hint of what was beneath. Or if his shirt was flung around his neck, exposing all the blond hair beneath. Another of her soft sighs threatened to turn into a moan. No, she decided, they were never going to marry. In fact, right now, she couldn't even get the man into her bed...

It was the wrong time for him to say ''A penny.''

"I think it's a thought I'd better keep to myself."

Using an index finger, he drew an X on his T-shirt, over his heart. "I promise never to intrude on a lady's secrets."

Their eyes caught, meshed and held. Her breath stilled, trapped in her throat. Even though she knew what the answer would be, and even though she knew it would hurt her feelings, she huskily said, "Do you want to come back to bed with me?"

His eyes said he wanted to. They were dark, narrowed, intent. His mouth said, "I don't think..."

Quickly lifting her finger, she pressed it to his lips, just for an instant. He caught her hand, loosely threaded his fingers through hers, then drew their joined hands to his chest, pressing hers to where he'd just drawn the X. Thankfully, her sharp inhalation wasn't audible, but the way he was holding her hand was somehow worse than a kiss. Or better. It was definitely more romantic. Kisses, she found herself thinking, were so much easier than this. Feeling strangely raw, her throat burned with a flood of unspoken words. Words such as love me. And please. And come to bed because I can't stand not to have you inside me another minute. "It's all right," she said. "No need to explain. I just thought..."

He looked as edgy as she felt, as if he was trying not to fidget or breathe too hard. "It's a good thought, Carla."

She guessed that meant he wanted her physically, but couldn't risk another involvement with her. She didn't blame him. When she'd left him at the altar, she'd embarrassed him in front of half of Pittsburgh. Still, she couldn't help the fact that her voice turned suggestively raspy. "Then keep it as a thought." After all, he hadn't offered an unequivocal "no."

He smiled then, just a slight twist of his beguiling mouth, and the light in his eyes was deep, like something shining out from within him. "Well," he said with a sexy tilt of his head, "you have been known to do some wild things with your thoughts, Carla."

He was referring to her erotic dreams. "I bet you can do some pretty wild things with yours, too."

"You know I can."

A truly unbearable second passed, and when he dropped her hand, she felt strangely bereft, as if it might be the very last time she'd ever touch him. Dammit, she wanted him! And as the only child of Mary and Larry DiDolche, she was used to getting her way! She forced herself to turn from Tobias and look at the picture again. "Maybe there's a passageway inside the apartment," she mused, returning to their conversation.

As he sidled close enough that their bodies connected, she felt her emotions soar, more so when she heard his words. "I guess we'll have to go look."

Trying to mask her surprise, she said, "You're coming with me?"

"Sure." His voice was studiously neutral. "It could be interesting."

Very, Carla thought. If Tobias was in tow, the first place she wanted to start searching for an access panel would be her bedroom.

VINCE GATO GRUNTED as he dropped to his knee on the hard wooden floor, using the edge of a screwdriver to pry up a loose board. Vaguely, he realized he should lose some weight, and cursed under his breath. Larry DiDolche had come in from Florida looking like the cat's meow. Vince was the same age, but Larry looked years younger. Vince had always been on the heavy side, of course, but since his wife's death, he'd taken to eating out, and now…

The thoughts flew from his mind, and his breath quickened as the wood came free. As always, his body tightened when he saw the glint of gold inside. His eyes darted from the keys to the belt itself. Excitement lifted his spirits. Greedily, he reached inside, his beefy fingers closing over cold metal. Like a woman, the object warmed to his touch….

A priceless treasure, he thought, and yet he kept it here, buried in the dirt. Somehow, that was exciting, too. All these glorious gems hidden from everyone but him! With a heave, he came to his feet, headed for the desk and seated himself. Then he simply looked at his prize, tracing his fingers slowly over each inch of the golden circle of the waistband.

He uttered a sensual-sounding sigh as he lifted the belt to the dim overhead light, turning it for better perusal, so that the bejeweled front piece glittered. It was just too bad he hadn't yet been able to steal the picture from the Sloane mansion. Hungrily, his eyes roved over each stone. Diamonds glistened like snow. Rubies called to him with seductive female voices. Emeralds shined with a light brighter than a noon sun.

"Ah," he whispered, his breath quickening. The entire gem-studded front piece was slightly cupped, its suggestive curvature perfect for a woman he could only imagine.

Truly, the chastity belt was an heirloom. Priceless,

it had also been worthy of a man's death. Yes, it was too bad that Vince hadn't managed to remove the picture of it from the Preservation Society's collection, at least not yet.

And now Carla DiDolche was sleeping at the clinic. He fought down a rising surge of panic. It was possible she'd find the picture and see...

He pushed away the thought. No...no one could ever discover his precious secret. She'd never know that the belt was real, or in his possession. Her memories would remain only what they were now...memories she thought were nightmares.

The treasure in his hands was his...all his.

It had been handed down by his great-great-grandfather. Just as during the Crusades, when it had protected a warrior's woman from rape while he was far from home, the belt continued to provide protection for the Gato family. If anything ever happened to the import business, they would have this to sell. No matter what happened—wars, natural disasters, deportation—the Gatos would thrive. Not that they'd ever had to remove so much as one stone....

Vince only wished his boys were more worthy. But they'd left the family business, and so he hadn't yet initiated them into the secret of the heirloom. Maybe he wouldn't do so until his deathbed.

Too bad they wouldn't appreciate the back story more. Vince smiled, thinking of his great-great-grandfather, Anthony. He'd been so crafty and smart. He'd been wiry, slight of build and sly as a fox, too. At least that was how the story went. On the night in question—a dark, stormy night in the 1880s as fate would have it—Vito Gambolini had brought the chastity belt to the basement of the import business. As a jewelry appraiser, he was to make sure that the seller had taken a fair price from Cornelius Sloane.

Anthony Gato, of course, had his own plans.

Dining with Carla's great-great-grandfather, Michael, as an alibi, Anthony had excused himself briefly from the DiDolche table, used the secret back staircase to re-enter his own business, and murdered Vito Gambolini. Once he'd hidden the precious artifact, he'd returned to dinner.

Cornelius Sloane could hardly have gone to the police. If he had, a further investigation might have uncovered the pornography collection in the steel baron's home. Not that the old man hadn't hired thugs to break into the import business and ransack it, in hopes of finding the belt. But they never had. And because Gambolini was a known gambler, even Cornelius Sloane began to assume that a creditor had done him in and taken the artifact.

The chastity belt had belonged to the Gatos ever since.

8

"NOW, NOW, Vince Gato," said Mary DiDolche, "I don't care how much you think you weigh. You're not leaving my dinner table until you've tried one of these cannolis."

Tobias watched as Vince leaned back in his chair, patted his bulging belly, then reached for one of the confections Mary proffered. "I guess I can start dieting tomorrow," agreed Vince, chuckling as he took a bite. "You talked me into it, Mary."

"How about you, Tobias?" asked Larry fondly. "Another?"

As Tobias shook his head, his knee slammed against Carla's. The sudden, jarring crack of bone meeting bone should hardly have been sexy, but a spray of tingles rapidly spread upward, teasing his thighs, then making his groin tighten. "Sorry," he murmured, quelling the urge to slide his hand over her bare knee for a quick caress.

"I'll live," she replied dryly.

Glancing around, Tobias wasn't sure he would. Everything surrounding him made his heart ache. Because Carla had called her folks from the clinic to say he was coming for dinner, Mary had assumed he and Carla were back together and had rushed to invite his parents for the meal. It had been a feast, too. They'd started with home-baked Italian bread dipped in spiced olive oil, which had been served with fresh tomatoes topped with mozzarella. Salads and veal Parmesan had followed, along with fresh Swordfish from Nicco's downtown in the Strip District. The scents floating on the air might have rivaled those on a street in Sicily.

Mary's table had mirrored the same old-world charm. Set on an upstairs balcony overlooking Liberty Avenue, it was covered with a stiff white tablecloth and linens. Bright red flowers Tobias didn't recognize—maybe poppies—were displayed in a squat crystal dish, their sprawling green leaves looking crisp, trailing across the cloth. Trouble was, the table itself was small, which meant they were all crowded around it: his parents and Carla's, along with Vince Gato and Carla's cousin, Carmine, who'd eschewed dessert and was still in the process of mopping tomato sauce from his plate with a hunk of bread that was nearly the size of one of his huge hands.

Mary clearly felt her nephew's bad manners were a testament to the superiority of her cooking abilities. "Eat up!" she enthused happily. "More bread?"

Unable to speak because his mouth was so full, Carmine merely shook his head before lifting a glass for a swig of the burgundy wine Vince had brought.

"Everything's just fabulous," commended Tobias's mother.

His eyes caught hers. She, like Carla, had dressed in a becoming shade of green, though her dress was more conservative, calf-length with a high neckline. As he took in the woman who'd given birth to him, whom so many people often said he favored, Tobias half wished she hadn't worn the dress. Since it was one she wore for special occasions—she'd bought it for his cousin Alison's wedding—he was pretty sure she'd meant to commemorate him and Carla being back together, which they weren't. He sighed. All the sly, speculative glances passing between the dinner party guests were starting to get on his nerves. He should have guessed this would happen. Mary had always been the consummate matchmaker.

His mother was no slouch, either. And her efforts tonight were a sore reminder of how things had changed when Carla had run back down the aisle. If anyone had questioned him that day, he'd have said that they'd have had at least two kids by now, maybe three, and a home of their own in the suburbs. He figured he'd be worrying about life insurance policies and saving for the kids' college educations even though they'd just be starting grade school.

But here he was, with his folks, dining at the DiDolches apartment, just as they had in the days when he'd first started dating Carla. Glancing beside him, he sucked in a breath. Carla was just as gorgeous as she'd been then, too. The soft, waning evening light became her. Just past her shoulder, he could see the coming night sky turning startling colors. It reminded him of how the sky had looked years ago, on June first, right before his and Carla's six o'clock wedding. He hadn't been given to poetic thoughts then—he still wasn't—but it was beautiful tonight, just like Carla. Hot pink and amber-gold stripes were zigzagging horizontally across a blue backdrop that had deepened to purple, the jagged strips looking like torn strips of kids' construction paper. Dark, pearly, purple-tinged clouds were starting to roll in from the east, and the great globe of the fiery bloodred sun dominated it all—inching ever so slowly over the horizon line and leaving fingers of red in its wake as if it were waving goodbye.

"Pretty, huh?"

Carla's voice was low and husky, and when he heard it, he cursed himself inwardly for being so relaxed. Just as that voice warmed him, moving through his bloodstream and making everything inside him turn creamy and hot, he realized he should have been bracing himself against his responses. But how could he? The other morning, the taste he'd gotten had revived feelings he'd long been denying…feelings that said he wanted her back. If only in his bed.

Glancing into her dark eyes, he realized she'd probably been watching him a long time. "Yeah, it's great to look at," he finally returned, his brown eyes narrowing as he surveyed her. He wondered if his tone revealed what he was thinking: that it was her, not the sky, that was breathtaking. He couldn't help but flick his gaze over her wild corkscrew curls. They were the color of wet jet-black ink and spiraled all around her face, framing full lips and high cheekbones, not to mention dark, flashing eyes that sparkled with sin. The dress was none too shabby, either, a short emerald silk number with spaghetti straps. It was cut just low enough, and he was just enough taller that he'd been offered a dynamite view of her cleavage all during dinner.

She'd caught him looking, too.

Over and over, as she'd moved this way or that, his eyes would follow greedily, his breath catching as the fabric peeled away from the sloping skin of her breast.

Each time, the liquid silk pulled back almost enough for him to glimpse her—

Almost, he'd think, his breath quickening and turning shallow as his groin got taut. Stupid, he thought now. Nothing more than a quick peek had gotten him so horny that he was about to lose his mind. He hadn't even been this susceptible to being flashed in junior high school. Now, he watched once more as the silk edged away, stopping when it was just a fraction from exposing the tempting sandy edge of a nipple. Oblivious, Carla shifted directions and obscured his view, leaving him to inhale sharply, pulling air through his clenched teeth.

Yeah, she was definitely driving him crazy. Soon, he'd be alone with her, too. And despite his every good intention, he was beginning to think that whenever he could shoo everyone out the front door, he'd drag her upstairs, rip off her clothes and savage her.

"When are we leaving?" Mary asked right on cue, as if she were intentionally helping him set the stage for seduction.

Lost in fantasy, Tobias could only blink. In his mind, he'd tucked his hands down the bodice of Carla's dress, pushed away the fabric so that her lush breasts were in his hands. They were so heavy as he tested their weight, the tips so firm, so ready for his mouth that Tobias had to bite back a groan—and only hope he wasn't expected to rise from the table anytime soon, given the intensity of his response. Jeans that had felt comfortably loose before now were starting to feel as painfully constricting as wet Lycra....

Larry was glancing at his watch. "As far as I'm concerned, we can take off anytime."

Tobias damned his mind for being so predictably male as it raced ahead, wondering whether or not Carla was still sleeping in her old bedroom. Not that he would act on his impulses, he told himself. When she'd invited him into bed before, he'd understandably weakened, but since then, the incident with Sloane Junior cost him the lease on the clinic. As Tobias's gaze slid to Vince Gato, he pushed away an unwanted sense of discomfort.

Then he tuned back into the conversation. "I've got to get back to the shop," Carmine was griping good-naturedly. He owned a locksmith business near the clinic. "Some of us have to work for a living. But where are you all headed tonight? Out on the town?"

Mary chuckled. "A Frank Sinatra look-alike contest and sing-along at the cultural center." She sent Laura and Jack Free a smile. "Are you all still coming with us?"

Tobias's mother grinned. "Of course. Wouldn't miss old Blue Eyes for the world."

"I think they're going to have some Tony Bennett's, too, right?" asked Vince.

"Yeah." Carmine tore off another hunk of bread. "Now that you mention it, I think I heard about this. Everybody dresses up and sings songs, right? Are you going, Vince?"

As Vince Gato nodded, a prickle raised the hairs on Tobias's arms. There it was again, he thought. That weird discomfort he sometimes felt around the man. Shrugging off the feeling, he reminded himself that Vince was a friend of the DiDolches. Besides, just being a member of the Preservation Society didn't make the man Satan incarnate. Still, the feeling lingered, and try as he might, he couldn't really put his finger on why. When another whiff of Carla's perfume claimed his attention, he pushed aside the uncharitable thoughts. His father said, "We really ought to push off. Should we take one car or two?"

"Oh, let's just take one," Mary rejoined swiftly. "There's room enough for us in Larry's Cadillac."

Larry, who couldn't have been more proud of his late model, bright red car, added, "There's room in that car for the whole neighborhood."

Carla laughed. "As much as you love that car," she said, "why don't you take it to Florida and off my hands?"

Larry had left it parked in a nearby garage and apparently, Carla had been driving it once a week for him. "What would I drive when I came home to see you, sweetheart?" Larry asked his daughter in a put-on James Cagney voice.

"You could rent a car," she suggested.

Larry looked appalled. "What?" he joked. "One of those little compact numbers?"

"God forbid," teased Mary.

Tobias's father sent Carla a warm smile that left no doubt as to how much the Frees wanted her back in their lives. "Well, as much as we hate to leave you and my handy son to clean up after us..." Jack's voice trailed off.

Tobias feigned a look of annoyance, but once more, his heart tugged in a way he'd prefer to ignore. Dammit, why did the two families have to hit it off so well? His and Carla's parents couldn't have been more different, of course. His were uptight WASPS who spent most of their spare time golfing. They were tanned, tall, blond and skinny as string beans, while the DiDolches were dark-skinned, lively and down-to-earth. Heavy around the middle, too, due to Mary's cooking, or at least they had been until Larry started his new health-club kick. Nevertheless, despite the differences, there had always been an inevitable feeling of rightness to how easily the two families spent time together.

"Don't stay out too late," Carla teased her parents as everyone rose.

"We won't," they promised.

"Hey, coz." As Carmine stood, a sleeveless undershirt rose on his taut belly, and rippling bare muscles moved making a tattoo—a cluster of purple grapes—jiggle on his biceps. "I'd stick around and help with the cleanup, but Theresa Giovanni called my cell when I was on my way over here. She says she needs a new deadbolt, pronto."

Just as Carla smirked, Tobias caught her gaze and chuckled softly. Partially because of Carmine's unusual attachment to his cell phone. And also because of his longtime attachment to Theresa Giovanni. She lived right around the corner and despite her three-year-long, volatile marriage to Dominick Mineo, she'd had a crush on Carmine since high school.

"What?" asked Carla. "Did she throw Dom out again?"

Carmine nodded, flashing his cousin a grin. "Yeah. So, after I change the lock…." He shrugged suggestively.

Larry elbowed him in the ribs. "Good boy." He winked at Carla. "It's in the genes," he said. "They don't call us Italian stallions for nothing. The women just can't keep their hands off us.''

Mary groaned.

''I do all right for a guy with an English pedigree,'' Tobias couldn't help but defend himself, but then he was sorry he had, since it only prompted another uncomfortable round of sly glances.

''On that note...'' Mary began as if to indicate that he and Carla were about to be alone.

Which they were just a second later. As soon as the room cleared, Tobias realized nothing was stopping him from suggesting they head straight to her bedroom. Except, of course, that he was never sleeping with her again.

Trying to divert his own attention, he glanced around as he began carrying some plates toward the kitchen. ''You've really made the place your own,'' he commented.

''You like?''

He nodded. She'd removed much of her parents' stuff, mostly things that had a decidedly 1970s flavor, in favor of comfortable, modern pieces of furniture. ''It looks a lot less like a *Brady Bunch* rerun.''

She laughed. ''The orange upholstery had to go.''

''Sometimes retro is okay.''

She came up behind him in the kitchen. ''Let's just leave that stuff for now,'' she suggested. ''I want to look around.''

''Let's at least bring the dishes inside,'' he returned, heading again toward the balcony and vaguely wondering if he and Carla would really find a hidden staircase. It seemed unlikely.

She sent him a smirk. ''You're so good.''

Hardly. Every time he looked at her in that sexy little green dress he wanted to tear it off her body with his teeth. His tone carried a faint hint of warning. "You know better."

She nearly bumped into him as she reached past him for the half-full bottle of wine. "Good stuff," she said approvingly, lifting the bottle, her eyes scanning the label.

It had come from the extensive collection of vintage bottles that Vince Gato kept in the basement of the import company. "Whoa. Let's keep that out," said Tobias as she moved to put it in the cupboard. Hooking his fingers around the bottle, he lifted it to take a swig. "Yummy."

Carla rolled her eyes. "What manners."

"Better than your cousin Carmine's."

She laughed. "I won't argue with that."

He offered the wine to Carla, and was somehow surprised when she took it, followed his lead and drank from the bottle. Usually, she was daintier and inclined to use wineglasses. When she lifted the bottle away from her lips, he had to fight an urge to swiftly lean and kiss her. The impulse was akin to a compulsion. Weakening, he decided her mouth was simply too wet and red to resist. Her voice was too throaty, also. She sounded exactly as she did in the moments after she'd climaxed. The words caught.

"What say, let's take the bottle down the hall," she murmured.

His eyes were still locked on her mouth. "Down the hall?"

"To my bedroom."

His lips parted involuntarily in surprise, at least until

she clarified by saying, "We were going to start looking for the staircase, remember?"

"Oh, right," he muttered. If there was a secret staircase, left here after all these years, the access was probably in Carla's bedroom. It sounded as if she might have found it during her nocturnal wanderings. "We should definitely start there."

She nodded. "Ready?"

"Sure." As he followed her through the living room, then down the hallway, he braced himself, but there was no stopping the unhindered trajectory of his gaze, which traveled over her bare shoulders, then down her curved spine, and settled on her twitching backside. It stayed there a very long moment.

When they were inside the bedroom, she turned around and caught him looking. Quickly he lifted his eyes, only to have them burn all the way up the front of her. Yeah, he thought. Carla DiDolche had a helluva body. Full curving hips that a man could grab onto. A waist his hands could circle.

She considered him a moment, then said, "I can't believe my parents listened to everything you said about the café."

Glancing around the bedroom, taking in every detail, he'd barely heard her. In a non sequitor, he murmured, "It looks the same." Maybe he shouldn't have said it. It was just one more reminder of the time they'd spent here years ago, cuddled on the queen-size bed while her parents were out for the evening. Just like tonight. Memories of a younger Carla washed over him. In high school, she'd worn her hair shorter, and she'd been taller than the other girls, embarrassed because of her well-endowed chest. She'd worn braces, too. And he'd never forget how they'd felt, scraping his sensitive flesh, the first time she'd gone down on him. Shuddering, he tried to push away the image, but it remained in his mind, along with all the tenderness he'd felt as he'd gently brushed back her hair, feeling insane with lust even as he'd tried to rein in his emotions and offer gentle encouragement.

She was eyeing him. "More or less," she agreed.

He had no idea what she was talking about. "Huh?"

"The room," she said, squinting at him quizzically. "It is the same, more or less. But I painted it peach."

"I remember," he managed. "It used to be pink."

She nodded. "Ma's idea."

"Very girly." He glanced at one of the walls where feathery light mint-green butterflies were visible on the peach background. "You did that?"

She nodded again. "As soon as I moved back in, I repainted, myself. Carmine helped. He redid the kitchen cabinets, too, and put a new sink in the bathroom."

Tobias was impressed. "It looks great. So does the café."

"Like I said at dinner, I could do a lot more, but you know how my parents are."

"You're right about making changes, though."

Now those kissable lips pursed. Right now, every move she made seemed like a beacon on a dark stormy night. "I don't know why they'll listen to you, but not me," she complained, her mind clearly on another wavelength.

The competitive edge to her voice made him smile. "They like me?" he couldn't help but suggest, shoving his hands into his jeans pockets as he teased her, and relaxing against the doorjamb.

Her jaw dropping in mock exasperation, she stared at him. ''They like me, too, Tobias. I'm their daughter!''

He merely sent her a long, sideways smile and shrugged. ''Maybe so, but when I talk, they do listen.''

''Rub it in.''

''Sorry, but they do.'' During dinner, when the subject of the café had come up, Carla had done her best to get her parents' blessing regarding the introduction of new coffees. She also wanted Carmine to build a patio so customers could be served al fresco, but only when Tobias entered the conversation did they really pay attention.

She was staring at him, her dark eyes now moody and unreadable. ''It's true,'' she said with a hint of surliness that was somehow utterly beguiling.

He merely chuckled. ''Now, don't pout.''

''But they don't listen to me.''

''Sure they do.''

''Not the way they do to you.'' Stepping around a bed piled high with pillows, she came toward him.

The closer she got, the more his relaxed muscles tensed. Usually, she didn't wear much perfume, but tonight he'd gotten a heady dose of something he'd never smelled before. It mixed with the scent of her skin in a way that was truly sinful. Spicy and hot, the concoction made him think of cinnamon and musk, and then suddenly, made him quit thinking altogether. ''Nice perfume,'' he murmured.

She looked pleased. ''You really like it?''

Dammit, rejecting this woman sure wasn't easy. Especially when he'd wound up in a bedroom with her again. ''Yeah. It's nice.'' Knowing he'd better switch the subject, he said, ''And your folks do listen to you.''

She stopped in front of him. Dangerously close from his humble point of view. ''Not the way they listen to you,'' she said.

He hardly wanted to contemplate the truth in it. Mary and Larry DiDolche each had a headful of old-world notions. Mass every Sunday, dinner at six, no sex before marriage. As far as they were concerned men, not women, wore the pants and made the decisions. Or at least a woman was supposed to make things appear that way. After all, Mary could make Larry do just about anything she wanted. Still, Tobias had been the son they'd always wanted and never had. He finally said, ''At least they agreed to let Carmine build a patio.''

Looking dissatisfied, Carla placed a hand on her hip in annoyance. The movement only served to pull the luscious silk fabric more tightly against her body. Another pang claimed his groin. This one was so swift and intense that Carla might as well have put her hand on his jeans and squeezed. Wincing against the unwanted sensation, he tried to avert his gaze, but couldn't tear it away from her. It traveled to where the hem had lifted inches higher on her smooth thigh, then shifted to where the fabric twisted at her waist. Pulled across a breast, he could see the beaded tip, a puckered indention that made his mouth water.

Suddenly, he wanted to taste her through the cloth, to tease her until she simply stepped back and undressed for him. Once, years ago, in this very room, she'd done a little striptease for him that he still used to excite himself on occasion. She'd been wearing her pep club uniform, knee socks and saddle oxfords, and once she'd undressed, she'd aroused him beyond compare with the pom-pom streamers. It was truly special, the kind of thing a guy didn't easily forget.

"You do want the patio built, don't you?" he managed to prompt, wishing they'd get moving and look for the fool staircase soon.

"Yes." Her gaze rose to meet his, and given the sudden, unmistakable flash of heat in the dark irises, she was sharing every sensual thought he was trying to submerge. He was pretty sure she meant for the word yes to pertain to countless things other than the patio.

Slowly, she lifted the wine bottle to her lips.

"I'll take another drink, too," he found himself saying.

When Carla flashed him a smile, he realized how dark it was getting. The last slivers of sun were weakly streaming through a window. Her voice caught. "Say please."

He was still leaning against the doorjamb, but nothing inside him felt as calm as he looked. Instead of moving, he sent her a long look from beneath his eyelids. "You want me to say please?"

Her answering smile was damnably alluring. "Pretty please," she said.

"You're really pushing it, DiDolche."

"DiDolche?"

He nodded. Just being in this room reminded him of their high school days, when he'd often called her by her last name.

Her smile broadened. Silk swished in the silence as she walked the few paces toward him and held out the bottle. "I like to live dangerously."

His eyes were hot on hers. "My, my. You really are pushing your luck."

"Care for a drink, sailor?"

Longing jolted through him, and a spark danced along his arm as their fingers touched. His throat tightened as he lifted the bottle to his own lips. As soon as his mouth touched the glass rim, it wasn't wine he tasted, but Carla. He knew he'd kiss her then. He had to drink in that succulent mouth just once more. Close his lips over the firm flesh of hers. He wouldn't make it through this night if he didn't. His heart hammered as he thought of getting naked with her, pushing each inch of his hard heat inside her. Just imagining the sensations—the slick burning feeling as she enveloped him in wet velvet—he felt as if he was drowning.

Sipping, he let the liquid slide slowly down his throat, warming his body in a room already made warm by the waning summer sun. When he brought the bottle back down, he realized her eyes were intent on his face. And she looked beautiful, too, more so than at dinner, the dusky light of the room suiting her, making her olive skin look darker, smoother.

"Look, Carla," he found himself saying. "I don't want to relive the past, if you know what I mean...." Hell, he thought when she nodded, why would Carla know what he meant? He didn't really know, himself, other than that he didn't want a replay of what had happened at the church seven years ago. He plunged ahead anyway. "I mean, I don't want to start a relationship."

Her lips were slightly parted, and he could swear he'd just heard her pant. "But?"

He stared at her another long moment, then he simply said, "Do you want to have sex?"

IF TOBIAS THOUGHT she was going to say no, or that she'd remind him they'd come into the bedroom to look for an access panel to an old secret staircase that probably didn't even exist, he was wrong. "Yeah," Carla said quickly. She'd thought he'd never ask. She'd been staring at him all during dinner, hoping that as soon as everybody left, they could...

He didn't look as committed as she felt. "I'm not kidding when I say I don't want to get involved," he clarified.

"Just sex," she agreed.

"Right."

She tried not to let it hurt her. Maybe it didn't, at least not when her gaze drifted down the front of the faded blue T-shirt he wore tucked into equally faded jeans. By the time she took in the inviting bulge beneath his fly, Carla was no longer worried about the relationship question. "Just sex," she whispered.

He didn't say anything. But then, he didn't have to. His body was doing all the talking. Beneath that zipper, he was definitely packing heat. Leaning, she aggressively molded her palm over the waiting mound, feeling warmth seep into her palm as she lifted to her tiptoes and closed her mouth over his. She squeezed tightly, her fingers pressing his erection, her heart swelling when she felt the urgency of his response. Stiffening completely under her touch, the mass gained definition beneath her trembling fingertips, the shaft and head easily outlined as she began stroking.

She felt a twinge of guilt, as if she was somehow forcing him. "Are you sure you want to do this?"

Any remaining doubts were gone. "Yeah."

Familiar heat washed over her body as his mouth started moving masterfully on hers. God, she missed this man. He knew exactly how to kiss her, how to move his body against hers. He was rolling his hips, using his to cradle hers. He remembered every trick she'd taught him years ago, and, no doubt, he'd learned some new ones.

"You feel good," he said simply, his hands sliding over her buttocks, curling over mounds of flesh. She felt so tiny as his long splayed fingers rose and completely circled her waist. So feminine. She seemed to shrink under huge hands as he hauled her closer, relocking their hips in the way she loved, angling his body to hers. He squeezed her hand out from between them, so she could feel his hard length when it settled on her cleft, opening her completely through her clothes.

Opening her mouth further, she invited his tongue, and he gave it, sliding it against hers, then against her slippery, smooth inner cheek. Exploring the crevices of her mouth, he kissed her as if he'd never done so before. Her palms flattened, gliding upward on the front of his shirt until her fingers found his taut nipples. Shuddering, she worried them with the friction of her palms, then plucked them between her fingers. His groan was lost in the kiss that carried the last vestiges of the warm red wine.

Shifting his hips, he further pressured her, and she gasped. He was so aroused. Her own nipples peaked and she brushed her chest to his, taut tips meeting taut tips. It was more than she could stand. She'd never wanted anything as badly in her life as she wanted this man.

Hooking her fingers into the front waistband of his pants, she kissed him once more. And then slid her greedy fingers between his flat, well-muscled stomach and the jeans, squeezing her own thighs together to stop the flood of moisture, not that it helped. She tugged him toward the bed. Against his mouth, she breathlessly said, "Let's get undressed."

His voice was husky. "You don't have to convince me."

"Hurry," she whispered.

"Do we have to?"

"Yes."

"Maybe the first time."

At the thought of a slow second time, she panted. "C'mon, Tobias."

Stepping away, she backed toward the bed again, pulling him, her eyes roving downward to settle below his belt. She flashed a smile made weak by desire. "I have condoms," she managed to say.

He grinned, his eyes narrowing, the irises so sexy that her knees weakened and she almost lost her footing. She tugged him yet another step toward the mattress and oblivion. Leaning away a second, he tugged the shirt from his waistband, pulled it over his head and tossed it to the floor, his eyes never leaving hers. "You do, huh?"

"Lots."

Chuckling softly as he playfully pushed her onto the bed, he asked, "Am I dreaming?"

He was referring to how he'd gotten into bed with her at the clinic, on the pretense they'd already made love. "Since you don't want to get involved again," she said, leaning fully back, her legs dangling over the side of the mattress, "we'll pretend this is a dream, okay?"

Gazing down at her, he edged closer. As he used a long-limbed muscular thigh to part hers, the hem of the emerald green sundress rose on her thighs. Opening a fraction further for him, she did her best to tease him with the visuals, letting the hem rise almost to her thong panties.

He lifted a bushy eyebrow, and when he spoke, his tone was barely audible, as charged with sex as the rest of him. "Given what you've told me about your dreams, I don't think I'll mind starring in one of them."

"Ah. I was considering only giving you a supporting role."

"No way baby. I'm the lead man."

He always had been. She loosed an audible sigh, parting her legs, just another mind-bending fraction, so he could have more access. This time, the panties showed. Just a hint. They were sexy panties, too. Of black velvet. Up top, the bra he hadn't yet discovered was just as alluring, a black string with tiny velvet triangles that stretched over nipples she felt tightening now, constricting painfully. She burned with arousal, responding to nothing more than the touch of his gaze and the anticipation of his hands.

"Take off your pants," she whispered.

"Demanding, aren't we?"

She smiled. "Not yet."

"I can't wait," he returned, opening his belt with one hand.

Her breath came out in a soft puff. "Me neither."

"I'll enjoy making you." Leather made a soft flapping sound as it fell away.

"Tease."

The snap to his jeans popped. "You love it."

"Show me."

"Are you watching?"

She was riveted. Her ears pricked at the metallic sound of the zipper coming down. When she hazarded a quick glance upward, his lips had twisted into that utterly irresistible smile she loved most, and his eyes had sharpened with awareness.

She glanced down again. "Ooh-la-la," she whispered, trying for humor that fell flat as he started sliding his jeans over his hips. Suddenly, she couldn't think of another thing to say. Or breathe. Or think. She widened her legs once more, inviting him closer still. He was so gorgeous. Long, hard, dusky.

His ragged voice made something deep inside her shake. "Where are those condoms?"

Her heart leaped in her chest, and she glided a hand over her own stomach, hoping to stop the butterflies that had just taken flight. Were she and Tobias about to have sex—real sex? Feeling his mouth on her this morning truly hadn't been enough. She needed so much more....

"Bedside drawer."

She glanced upward as a low chuckle sounded. "What?" she whispered.

"Looks like condoms aren't the only thing you've got."

Flames ate up her cheeks, and she winced, thinking of the vibrator. ''You weren't supposed to see that.'' Heaven help her if Tobias ever guessed she'd thought of him when she was using it.

''Maybe we can use it together,'' he murmured.

The thought was enough to send pure fire flooding into her veins. ''Right now,'' she murmured as he came back to the bed, ''I want the real thing.''

He shot her the world's sexiest smile. ''It doesn't get any more real than this.''

Leaning, he glided a hand along her thigh, pushing her dress higher still. She shuddered as he discovered the panties, running his palm over the velvet, stroking her with his fingers and discovering how damp she was.

Lifting and twisting her hips, she silently begged for more, relieved when he used the pad of his thumb to trace her clitoris through velvet. Feverishly hot, she strained and sighed when his whole hand covered her. Just when she felt she couldn't take any more, he increased the pressure, urging her to move with the rhythm as he rocked the heel of his palm against her. Perspiration beaded on her upper lip. She was going to come, and Tobias hadn't even removed her clothes yet. ''Yes,'' she whispered.

''No,'' he teased.

''Yes,'' she persisted.

''No,'' he said, loving her with his touch.

''Now,'' she demanded.

She groaned as he stripped the scanty thong down her thighs, tossing it in the direction of his discarded shirt. ''I think I'm about ready to make use of one of those foil packets,'' she whispered shakily.

"I'll bet."

Lifting on her elbows, she tugged the dress over her head. She couldn't have been more satisfied when he stared at what remained of her underwear. Yes, the bra thankfully took his breath. Now that she was naked, save for the two teensy triangles of black velvet over erect nipples, they were even. Hopefully, this would push him into further action....

"Carla," he said simply, his tall, lithe runner's body bending like a bow as one of his hands curled over her thigh. The other lifted to her shoulder, offering a slow caress. As he hooked a finger under a bra strap, his eyes glazed. He traced a black triangle, outlining its contours, then he tweaked the nipple. Desire wracked through her system like a sob, and her mind blanked as she shut her eyes. Didn't he know how much she wanted him? She was creaming. Every inch of her flesh was hungry with waiting.

"What do you want me to do first?" he whispered.

That was her Tobias. "Screw me," she whispered.

"What language," he chided.

"Please."

"I think something can be arranged."

She could feel his unsheathed burning heat gliding up her thigh. "Quit teasing me."

Low and sexy, his voice took on a needy edge as he unhooked her bra from the back and drew the straps down her arms. "I'm not teasing," he assured. And he wasn't. His eyes were dark and smoky. Deadly serious.

"Oh," she managed as both those big hands closed over her breasts. Whimpering, she enjoyed the dazzling sensations as he stroked them all over, swirling his fingers over her flushed skin, touching everywhere but the still painfully aroused tips. Thrusting her chest, she uttered soft whinnies as his long warm fingers stroked the undersides, then crested over the tops. Reaching, she circled her arms around his neck, trying to draw him closer, until he kissed her again.

His lips were so hard and passionate, so wet with abandon. Brazenly, his tongue pressed deep between her lips, its tip tussling, just as the hot tip scalding her thigh edged closer to where she was aching for him.

His fingers found her nipples, making her think he was never going to stop torturing her. But no…he was. He was between her legs now. Using his penis, he readied her, stroking her with it, parting her until she gasped, "Please. Oh, please."

Hovering over her, his free hand simply continued rolling a nipple between fingers he'd dampened with her moisture. He was rubbing and pinching until every inch of her ached, until everything inside her was taut, until her buttocks tightened, pushing…pushing…

Against her opening, he was throbbing. "I thought we were supposed to be looking for a secret passageway," he whispered.

"I have a secret passageway."

"I can see." Bracketing her open thighs with his hands, he thrust inside. Pleasure flooded her as she felt each ridge. He hadn't used the condom, after all. Quickly, she climbed. Waves of heat tumbled over her.

His mouth found hers, his lips as unforgiving as the hands molding over her breasts while his length went all the way to her womb and she let him rip through her.

She soared to heaven with white clouds and angels,

then dropped to hell where all was dark and wicked. And then she was home again. On Liberty Avenue. In her own bedroom. With Tobias.

And it felt as if they'd never been apart.

9

"HERE IT IS! I can't believe this!" Carla exclaimed nearly two hours later as she finished prying off a panel inside her bedroom closet. Setting aside the slab of wood, she shined a flashlight's beam inside, hesitated, then stepped through the opening. "Tobias!" she continued, craning her head to look at him. "I never really thought we'd find anything!"

"Me, neither." He'd figured the passageway would dead end. "Can you stand up in there?"

"Not yet."

He shook his head in surprise. Maybe there was a secret staircase, after all. Ducking, he squeezed inside the closet, catching a whiff of Carla's scent as he pushed back a rack of clothes to make more room for himself. Pausing, he breathed in deeply, letting the enticing smell of her mix with the scent of lovemaking that was still on his skin. He'd missed her. Maybe he hadn't really known how much until tonight. An image of her fleeing the altar went through his mind as it had so many times, but he pushed it away. He didn't want to ruin the closeness they'd just shared by dwelling on the past again. Especially not now, when they might have found the old staircase. Peering into the hole in the wall, he could see only darkness, and his heart missed a beat. It was as if she'd vanished forever.

"Are you still in there, Carla?" Of course she is, he thought, feeling foolish.

"Yeah." Her disembodied voice floated to him. "I can't believe this doorway was in my bedroom all this time. I never knew."

"You must have," he countered. "At least on some level." After all, she'd walked right to it, once they'd gotten dressed and started looking.

"I did come straight to it, didn't I?"

"That probably indicates you have an implicit memory of it."

"Ah, Dr. Free," she chided. "You're getting technical on me."

He chuckled, remembering how much he'd always loved talking shop with her. "It means you remember, but not consciously. The memories are evident only from your behavior."

"Wouldn't I have remembered before now?"

"Probably not. Implicit memory is often cued from clues in the environment. People go years without remembering things, then suddenly, they'll read a book or film where their situation is depicted, and everything will come back to them."

"Hmm. I think I have implicit memories of your body, Tobias."

He laughed. "It felt like it."

"Ever have sex in a secret passageway?"

"Not yet."

"Good answer." Suddenly, her voice quivered. "I hope there aren't any...critters in here."

It didn't sound as if she'd gotten very far away from him. She was only a few feet inside. "Do you see any stairs?"

"No. Maybe it's just a crawl space. It's dusty back here."

His throat tightened with uncharacteristic emotion at the easy conversation. He couldn't believe he and Carla were speaking again. Not to mention sharing over-the-top sex. Crouched in front of the access panel, he traced his eyes over the perimeters. The opening was about four feet tall by two feet wide. If he folded himself in half, Tobias figured he could get inside. Now he could see Carla's figure receding into the darkness. She'd gone about four feet. "Can you see anything now?"

Light bobbed from the flashlight. "Not really."

"I'm coming in."

"Watch out," she warned, casting the weak beam in a circle.

"Too bad there wasn't another flashlight," he complained, since she'd found only one in the kitchen.

"There's not much room in here, Tobias." She loosed a low whistle. "Directly beneath us is the bathroom in the café, so I always thought the panel in the closet was for the plumbing."

"I guess your subconscious knew better."

"Wouldn't I have looked before now?" she asked again.

He shook his head. "No. Especially not if the passageway led somewhere scary. If you came down here when you were a little kid, you might have blocked it from your mind."

Her voice, so husky with arousal as they'd twined their limbs together under the sheets, was now tentative. "I wonder where this leads?"

"We'll see." Tobias crouched inside the space.

"Unbelievable," he whispered, his hands out, a chuckle passing his lips when he ran into Carla. Gently, he molded a hand over her backside and kept it there, making an aren't-you-yummy sound.

"I should have told you to stay back there," she griped.

"I like it when you can't defend yourself."

He felt her hand settle over his fly. "Now, who can't defend themselves?"

"Who wants to?"

Knowing there was no way she could turn around, not even to give him a good-natured swat, he glided his hand under her dress to caress her more intimately, pleased when she released another sigh. "Quit," she murmured.

Just as his hand widened, splaying on her thigh, her voice hitched excitedly. "The tunnel's opening out. Isn't this incredible! I can't believe I have a secret passageway in my apartment. This is almost as wild as what you found over at the Sloane mansion."

And almost as wild as the hand moving on her warming flesh. "Tobias," she whispered in warning. Just then, the flashlight went out. "Drats," she added, hitting it against her palm, judging from the sound.

"What?" he teased, using his hand to guide her toward him in the darkness. "Are you afraid?"

"Yes. Actually I am. Just a little."

"Given your nightmares, I can see why."

Nevertheless, she laughed as he roughened the soft skin of her cheek with his five o'clock shadow. "Obviously," she whispered, "there's some sort of sex goblin in here."

Just as his mouth missed hers—landing just to the

left of her nose—he drew a sharp breath. Suddenly, he wanted her so badly that he knew they'd have to do it right here. As his lips found their mark, parting hers to find waiting dampness, he bent his knees, dipping to kiss her neck. As her silken hair tumbled over the back of his hand, he stroked the fingers upward, grabbing the strands and guiding her mouth.

Yes, she was kissing him as if he still belonged to her. And maybe he did. In some primal, elemental way, he figured he and Carla would never stop needing each other. Pushing his tongue deeper inside her mouth, he probed, licking around the rims of her teeth.

"We can't," she panted. "Not in here. Not in the dark."

Taking the flashlight from her hand, he placed it on the floor. "Why not?"

Before she could answer, his mouth was on hers again. It came down hard, but immediately softened as he pushed her dress up, then reached between them, undoing his jeans.

"Cobwebs," she whispered raspily. "Dust. Mice."

"Lust," he countered raggedly.

She gave in. "You've got a point there, Tobias."

"Here," he murmured, blinking in the dark, hoping to glimpse her face as he molded a hand over the warmth of her backside, lifting her to him, impaling her the second after her feet left the floor.

"Ah," she whispered as he slid deeper inside her, melting like butter.

Cradling her head, he did his best to shield her from the exposed boards behind her. "Easy," he whispered, dipping lower to push inside her, his eyes shutting. Darkness folded into darkness as descended into what seemed a never-ending night. He quickened, his breath coming faster as joyous spasms wracked her, the maddening palpitations sweeping away the last of his control.

"That was fast," he whispered.

"Good," she countered as he lowered her to the floor.

He heard her shimmy the silk dress downward on her thighs, then search in the dark for her underwear. "Effective," she murmured.

"Always."

"Ready to see where my secret passageway leads?"

"To heaven," he assured her, refastening his jeans, then searching for the light.

"Can you find it?"

"Got it." After he tapped the light against his palm, hoping to make it work, he tried opening it and repositioning the batteries. The watery stream of yellow light came back on, its ray just strong enough that Tobias could make out hints of the dusty space. Carla was right. Cobwebs were everywhere.

"Good thing the flashlight went out," she whispered.

Smiling, he raised his gaze to eyes that looked doubly dark in the blackness of the cramped space they shared. "Why?"

She smiled back. "Because I'd never make love in here if I could see the place."

Make love. He liked the sound of it more than he wanted to admit. Moments ago, when he'd been buried deep inside her, he'd tried to tell himself it was just sex. Nothing special. Just an itch to scratch. A primal male urge to conquer. A hot quickie that would snuff out like a candle flame on a breezy night. But he knew better. Now that Carla was back in his life, he wasn't going to be able to let go. He couldn't stay with her, either, of course. Not after what she'd done. Her voice drew him from his reverie. "Tobias?"

He raised an eyebrow. "Hmm."

"Are you going to stand there all day?"

The lopsided tilt of her mouth made her look particularly girlish. Like a thousand things tonight, including her wanting body, it reminded him of their teenage years. "No," he said, moving forward.

Silence fell as they continued walking, then she said, "Stairs. They're really here."

"Looks like it." Edging protectively in front of her, he swung the flashlight's beam in arcs, searching for any debris on which she could stumble.

"Listen," she whispered.

As they continued down, he could hear voices coming through the walls. "Must be from the jewelry store next door to your place." When he felt her hand settle on his back, then grab a fistful of his shirt, he added, "You okay?"

"A little scared," she admitted.

"Do you remember coming down here?" When she said nothing, he continued. "Do you want to stop? We don't have to keep going, you know. I can come down here alone."

"No. That's okay. I just..."

"I'll go back to the room with you, then come down myself."

"No," she repeated. "I want to go."

Her voice was weaker now, and when he registered how much of the punch had gone out of it, he wanted to turn around and take her into his arms again. She sounded scared as hell. Just as in the old days, it made him feel a surprising rush of anger. He'd kill anyone who ever hurt her. Trying to keep his voice neutral, he prompted, "Just what, Carla?"

When they'd almost reached the bottom of the stairs, she stopped in her tracks. "I don't know," she whispered. "Maybe we should stop here, after all."

He turned then, surveying the face he could barely see in the dark. Before he thought it through, he whispered, "C'mere, sweetheart." Reaching an arm around her upper back, he drew her against his chest and wrapped her in a warm embrace. She melted against him. His voice was so husky that they might have been making love. "What's going on in that pretty little head of yours?"

Tilting up her head, she gazed into his eyes. "I don't know—" Her voice was hushed, as if she expected someone to hear them. "But it all seems so familiar now. I'm sure I was in here, Tobias. I think I was sleepwalking and woke up..."

Drawing her closer, wanting her to register the strength he carried in his limbs, he brushed a kiss across her forehead. "How old do you think you were?"

Shutting her eyes, she tried to remember. "I don't know. Maybe three. That's how it seems." She released a soft sigh. "I think I was standing right here when I started searching for a light switch. Do you remember how I said I ran my hand over the wall, looking for it?"

He managed a nod. He could barely stand to think of a three-year-old Carla lost down here in the dark.

"Yeah," he said, not bothering to fight the concern in his voice. "Do you want to go back to your room now?"

"No. Let's keep going. I'm okay."

"You're sure?"

"Yeah."

"We're almost to the bottom." Taking the lead, he reached behind him, grasping her hand. Somehow, he wasn't surprised when her fingers twined, threading between his. Dammit, no woman had ever made him feel so necessary. Suddenly, he came up short and cursed inwardly. "Looks like the stairs dead end."

Her voice caught. "They can't."

"Why not?"

"I just...know they don't."

Squinting, he looked at her over his shoulder. What he saw was enough to stop his heart. In the faint light, she looked astonishingly vulnerable. Her cheeks were as pale as alabaster. Her eyes looked wide and worried. Quickly, he glanced away. Her expression reminded him too much of how she'd looked on their wedding day, right before she ran. "Do you remember something else?"

Reaching, she took the flashlight from his hand and began to cast its ray around the passageway. Exposed beams ran from the ceiling to the floor, and the stairs themselves were rough-hewn, full of splinters. "Here," she murmured. Stepping closer to the wall, she ran her fingers over the wood. "It's another access panel. Like the one upstairs."

"I'll be," he whispered, leaning to help her. Using his fingers, he pried it loose. But instead of popping out, it swung open. "This one's got hinges," he said.

Carla was peering over his shoulder. "Where are we?"

Wherever they'd landed, the light inside was on. It was faint, its yellow color just about as uninviting as that transmitted by the flashlight. "Probably the Gatos' place," he guessed, nearly bumping into a furnace. As he stepped around it and further into the room, he grabbed Carla's hand again, offering support. As her fingers curled gratefully over his, he glanced around. "Do you recognize anything?"

Her voice was strangely muffled. "I do. I really do."

IT WAS THE BASEMENT from her dreams. "Why didn't I realize it was Gato and Gambolini's?" she whispered. Shouldn't she have known? But then she'd never been down here, not that she consciously recalled. She tried to think back...to pinpoint the exact day and time that she had last visited the basement, but she couldn't. Maybe she'd never been here, except in her nightmares...or whenever she'd stumbled down the old staircase. She glanced around, her eyes darting suspiciously into each murky corner.

Only then did she realize her heart was hammering, and she couldn't have been more glad for Tobias's hand. For a moment, his warm, strong fingers seemed to be the only thing anchoring her to the world. Without them, she felt as if she might simply rise from the floor, her feet lifting magically from dirty tiles as she began to float away.

"You've been down here?" he prompted.

She managed a nod. She just didn't know when. It could have been centuries, or a year, or yesterday. "I think maybe in grade school." She squinted. Somehow, things didn't quite make sense. It was as if a missing piece of her memory was just out of reach and yet refused to slide into place, so that she could…

What? Frustrated, she drew in a sharp breath, bringing with it the scent of dust and old wine, which was kept on shelves around the room's perimeters…

The desk.

Her eyes riveted on it. It was big, the wooden top to it old and scratched. "That's so weird," she whispered, almost doubting her sanity.

Tobias edged closer, and she pressed herself against his side. "What?"

She shrugged, her eyes piercing the gloom for clues. "I must have found the passageway and come down here as a kid," she said. "I must have seen someone holding the chastity belt…."

"An artifact that's somehow connected to the Sloanes," he added.

"Right," she continued. "But the weird thing is that, when we first came down here, I didn't immediately recognize the desk. I've seen it a thousand times in my memory, and yet, it took me a minute to…" Blowing out a shaky sigh, she shook her head in confusion.

"To pull it all together?" he finished. "And remember that this desk really is the one you saw in your dream?"

She nodded. "Obviously a memory," she corrected.

Slipping his arm around her, he brought her closer against his side. "It makes sense," he assured her. "Traumatic memories aren't stored in your mind in the regular way."

"No?"

He shook his head as he rubbed a palm downward on her side to comfort her. "No. Which is why they're so hard to figure out. In fact, a lot of them appear as dreams."

Well, this was definitely no dream. Carla swallowed hard, wondering who had threatened her. It seemed unbelievable that anyone associated with the Gatos would have done so. But why would someone else be in their wine cellar? "Who do you think I saw?"

"You can't remember anything new?"

She shook her head. "I'd realize it if it was someone I knew, wouldn't I?"

"Not necessarily. You didn't recognize the desk for a minute. In fact, chances are, if it was someone you knew, you might be less likely to remember because the incident would have been more traumatic."

She tried to suppress a shudder. Her usually tidy, predictable world seemed to be tilting on its axis. She realized Tobias was squinting down at her. "Hmm?"

"Whatever happened to Gambolini?"

"Who?"

"Gambolini," he said. "The partner."

"Good question." Such an obvious one, in fact, that Carla had never thought to ask it. As far as she knew, the Gatos had always been in business for themselves. After Vince retired, it was generally assumed that one of his kids would return to run the place. "Dad will know," she added. "We can ask him when he gets home. You know how he is about the history of Italians on the block and—" Suddenly gasping, she squeezed her arm tightly around Tobias's waist as she leaped backward, toward the access panel. "Somebody's coming!"

Overhead, heavy footsteps scraped across the wooden flooring. And then, at the top of a short flight of stairs, which were positioned across the room, a door creaked.

Just as it swung open, they fled.

"WE MADE IT." Breathlessly, her heart still beating hard, Carla collapsed onto the bed as soon as they reached her bedroom. As unsettled as she felt, Tobias felt good crushed on top of her. Protective. Sure, he was having second thoughts about their renewed contact, and she hardly blamed him, but she needed him. Her arms wrapped around his waist, hugging him tightly, and as his legs bracketing where hers dangled over the mattress, she burrowed her face against his neck.

"Still scared?" he whispered. As he threaded his fingers into her hair, he pulled in a shuddering breath as if just touching the strands could arouse him beyond compare. And maybe it could, she thought, her skin turning feverish when she felt the beginning of another erection. It brought a smile to her lips, even though their trip to the Gatos' basement had been more than disturbing.

"How could I be scared?" she asked. "With you on top of me?"

His lips stretched into a smile that didn't meet his eyes. They looked concerned, serious. "That does the trick, huh?"

"Yeah."

Her throat grew tight. Suddenly, she couldn't speak.

Were they really here? In her bed? Shutting her eyes, she breathed in his scent as if for the last time. For weeks after she'd left him at the altar, she'd thought of such things: the last time she'd threaded her fingers through his chest hair. Or nibbled his neck. Or licked her tongue into his belly button. She'd marveled through her tears, wondering how she could have done those things not knowing it was the very last time....

Now, for a second, she simply soaked in the feel of him, the pressure of his long-boned thighs against hers, the jut of a knee locking to hers, the dizzying caress of those strong fingers as they combed her hair. And then she opened her eyes again. His were warmer, more softly brown than she'd ever seen them, and in the dark room, with only a light shining from the hallway, the angles of his face looked more prominent, making his features more intense.

Ever so gently, he began using the back of his hand to push the hair from her face, brushing the strands away from her temples, as if he wanted to better see her eyes. "You want to talk about what happened down there?"

What happened was that Tobias had played the role of her male protector to the hilt, and she'd loved every minute of it. "I'd rather not...not right now." Not when he was lying on top of her again.

"You probably should."

She sent him a mock pout. "Ah," she murmured, still gazing upward, not lifting her gaze from his. "Whatever the doctor orders."

As he shifted his weight, she felt her chest constrict. Heat poured into her, rising from beneath the fly of his jeans; she felt the ridge harden, the flex of it taking her breath. "All right," he conceded, his voice turning husky once more. "I guess you can have a little medicine."

"Kiss me," she whispered.

"Sure."

She loved the way he said it, as if kissing her were the easiest thing on earth, as if he'd never stopped doing so. Even more, she loved how his mouth felt. It barely grazed her lips, brushing gently back and forth, its touch firm, yes, but magical and feathery, too. She could feel it growing warmer with each pass. By the time his tongue traced slowly around her lips, drawing over each contour, her heart was fluttering like the wings of a bird.

"Kiss me harder," she whispered.

"Sure," he whispered again.

He was increasing the pressure of his mouth—just slightly, just enough to drive her mad with desire—when the exterior door to the apartment opened. Quickly, Tobias rolled away. Just as she grabbed the hem of her dress and yanked it downward, toward her knees, her mother waltzed in and flicked on the light switch.

"Carla? Are you in here? You're never going to believe it, but your cousin Carmine showed up, after all. And your dad won the Frank Sinatra New York, New York, sing-a-like contest. Jack joined in on the chorus and—" Mary drew a quick, surprised inhalation. "Oh, Tobias!" she exclaimed, putting out a staying hand as if to stop traffic. Her dark eyes, so like her daughter's, calmly took in the mussed bedding. "So sorry!" she managed. "I certainly didn't mean to interrupt."

"Interrupt what?" asked Larry, coming up behind his wife.

"They're in here necking." Mary shot her husband a long, sideways glance as he, too, took in the scene.

"Well," he offered philosophically, "it's your apartment now, Carla."

She was stunned. Her parents were firm believers in never having sex before marriage. "We weren't…" There was no use finishing the sentence. Both her parents looked as pleased as punch. Sitting up in bed, she tried to look as dignified as possible.

"We'll just leave you two alone," said her mother with a chuckle. "As long as Tobias promises to cook us breakfast."

Heat warmed Carla's cheeks to the point that she was fairly sure they were turning crimson. Were her parents really suggesting Tobias stay the night? "He wasn't…" she began again, unable to hide her shock.

"Oh, yes, he is."

Tobias's voice had sounded from beside her. She could merely stare at him. Before she could respond, he continued, "Before you go, Carla and I were just wondering about a piece of Liberty Avenue history. We were curious about what happened to Mr. Gambolini."

Larry leaned against the doorjamb. "What brings this up?"

Tobias shrugged. "We were talking about the neighborhood."

That was enough to satisfy her father, who loved to reminisce about history every chance he got. Just as Mary skedaddled in the other direction—she didn't share her husband's hobby—Larry said, "He was murdered."

"Murdered?" Scooting closer to Tobias and straightening her shoulders, Carla squinted at her dad. "How?"

"He was found in the basement of Gato and Gambolini's years ago. He'd been strangled. Oh..." Her father leaned farther back, shoving his hands deep into the pockets of a black sport coat as if that might, somehow, help him better remember. "It was back in the 1880s," he continued. "Not long after our businesses opened. It wasn't just an import business back then. That was the Gatos' contribution. The Gambolinis were relatives by marriage, and they had a sideline, importing old artifacts."

Carla glanced toward Tobias, and they exchanged a quick look. "Artifacts?" he asked.

Larry nodded. "Jewelry, too. Gambolini did a lot of appraisal work. He was the most reliable person around when it came to having an eye for precious gems. The ladies, too. And he was a gambler. Everybody figured one of his creditors did him in, so the case was quickly closed."

Carla considered. "They never caught the murderer?"

Just as his wife called to him from the other room, Larry shook his head. "No. Like I said, he'd been strangled, and they figured it was one of his creditors. They found him slumped over an old desk."

"An old desk," Carla echoed, instinctively knowing it was the same one that remained in the basement today. She started to ask her father if he'd known about the staircase, but then decided to refrain for now.

"Larry—" Mary's voice rang out. "Why don't you leave those two alone?"

Chuckling softly, Larry grinned. "Duty calls."

Before Carla could protest, the door shut. At least her parents hadn't gotten so suggestive that they'd turned out the lights, too. She looked beside her, at Tobias again, then gave in as he curled a hand around her shoulder and urged her to lie back on the mattress.

"I think they really want me to stay the night, Carla."

"What do you want?"

"To kiss you again."

"Then maybe you should."

She'd barely voiced the words before his mouth was on hers. This time, it took possession, the lips quickly claiming. The kiss did all the talking, too, saying he absolutely intended to take her folks up on their invitation. "I can't believe they said you could stay," she murmured against his mouth.

"They like me."

"I like you."

He chuckled softly, his mouth turning harder on hers, firmer. "Like me more."

His hand caught the hem of her dress and pushed it toward her thighs. Before he reached the leg band of her panties, she was damp for him again. "Remember when we were in high school," he added. "How we used to come in here?"

"Our hormones were out of control."

He laughed. "And they're in control now?"

"Maybe not."

She opened for him, parting her legs so he could slide easily between them. Instead, he leaned back and stripped her panties down her thighs for the third time this evening. With a shiver, she drew a breath between her teeth, anxious to feel his hands on her breasts again; they ached so. She hadn't bothered to put her bra back on, and now, her nipples were beading in painful knots. How could silk feel so abrasive? she wondered, relieved when he helped her remove her dress again. Sighing, she shut her eyes in wonderment as his mouth locked to a hardened tip. He suckled—his teeth scraping, his lips pulling. She threaded her splayed fingers through his hair and drew his head closer to her chest, whispering, "Tobias."

"What?"

Her voice was barely audible. "Don't stop."

"I haven't started yet," he promised. Ridding himself of his jeans, he rose from bed, just long enough to turn out the light. And then he was beside her again. Another minute passed, and he was inside her, his body moving with hers.

"We have to be quiet," she whispered.

"Very," he whispered back.

And they were.

10

"ARE YOU REALLY GOING to fix breakfast for my folks?" Carla asked the next morning as the first hints of sunlight streamed through the window.

Glancing downward, taking in the dark curls spread on his chest, Tobias leaned and brushed a kiss to her hair. "Doubtful," he murmured, flexing his legs and enjoying how hers twined around them. "I think that would be a bit much for me."

She laughed. "They can handle it, and you can't?"

"Basically."

She looked delighted. This morning, her skin looked like something out of a storybook. It should have belonged to a fairy princess, he thought. Smooth and satiny, it glided along every inch of him like running water. Pure summer seemed to seep from her pores, and as he slowly stroked her hair, then slid his palm down the long arching curve of her spine to her backside, he shut his eyes and drifted, lazily caressing the cheek of her bottom, swirling his hand over her responsive flesh.

She giggled. "You always were a butt man, Tobias."

"Breasts," he countered.

"Lips," she whispered back, kissing him.

He nudged her. "Knees."

"Toes," she returned sleepily, using hers to caress the top of his bare foot as she snuggled the sheet up around her shoulders.

"I like the whole woman," he found himself assuring her, pressing his head more deeply into one of her pillows and reveling in the feel of it, since it was stuffed with goose down.

"Do you?" Using her fingertips to tantalize him, she raked them between his pectorals, creating rivulets in his chest hair. Telltale bands tightened around his chest as her finger shifted directions and traced circles around one of his nipples.

When he finally spoke, his voice was throaty with sleep and arousal. "I'm starting to like the whole woman very much."

As her breasts beaded against his skin, their lovemaking became a foregone conclusion. Yes, it promised to be a glorious, sunny day. Better yet, since it was going to start with sex. Or at least he hoped so. Unfortunately, she seemed oblivious again, and when he glanced down, he realized her attention had shifted to the closet. "I can't believe we found a hidden staircase," she began, raising onto her elbow to get a better look at him.

He tried to grab her hand and pull her back downward. He'd much preferred what her fingers were doing just a moment ago, but she remained pensive.

"I was thinking..." she began again.

His every male instinct rebelled. "You look too gorgeous to think."

Not the least offended, she returned a wicked glance. "Really?"

He smiled lazily. "Yeah."

The morning light was doing wonderful things to her skin. The sheet had fallen away from rounded shoulders, and they glowed as if her body was lit from within. Reaching, he gently pushed the sheet further back to glimpse her breasts. Something dangerous swam into his bloodstream.

"Did you dream last night?" he asked.

When she shook her head, her curls bounced. "No..." She squinted. "Well, yes." Suddenly, she shrugged. "Maybe."

He chuckled softly, relieved. If she'd had nightmares, she would have remembered, or worse, she'd have been awakened by them. "Sounds definite," he teased.

Tilting her head, she continued surveying him, and when she didn't speak immediately, he stretched to deliver a slow, relatively chaste kiss. As he drew away, she said, "I didn't have any of the nightmares, but when I woke up, I was thinking things over. There has to be a connection between the watercolor we saw at the Sloane mansion and the genuine article."

"Which you saw in the Gatos' basement?"

She nodded, musing. "I guess I really did see a man down there years ago, holding it up to the light. Which means that, most likely, Gambolini was the appraiser for the chastity belt."

"Or the clearing house for it."

Edging downward, she curled her head on his chest again. "I mean, Gato and Gambolini's is a thriving business," she continued thoughtfully. "And before Gambolini was murdered, their trade involved artifacts."

"It's possible Gambolini bought the chastity belt to resell it, then kept it for himself."

"Doubtful. He was a gambler, remember? He was up to his eyeballs in debt."

"True. Maybe the chastity belt belonged to Cornelius Sloane."

"That would explain why he had a picture of it in his art collection," she agreed.

"Or maybe he saw the picture, then tried to purchase the belt." Stroking a hand down her back once more, he chuckled. "You'd look good in it, Carla. Just so you know."

"If we find it, maybe I'll model."

"I didn't know you were involving me in a mystery. Are we looking for it?"

"Of course."

Rather than responding, he slid a hand beneath her and simply scooped her up, so that she landed on top of him. "Here," he murmured, pulling away the sheet that bunched between them, then sighing when skin met skin. He shifted his weight, stirring his own raw hunger as he opened his legs so hers could fall between them. Each time she breathed, she chafed against him, the friction welcome and bothersome, by turns.

"I'm going back down there," she said, as if oblivious of his arousal. "I want to look around, to see if I remember anything else."

Judging from the hints of blue starting to peek through her curtains, he was going to have to get to the clinic soon. Even though Sloane Junior was snapping the place out from under him, he didn't intend to give up without a fight. Nor was he going to let his employees see him get demoralized. Now, more than ever, they needed to see him at work. "I don't want you going alone."

Only the sensual glint in her eyes assured him that she felt his erection now. Her lips were as soft as the goose down under his head, her tongue as silken as the hair tumbling onto his forehead. She kissed him as if they had all day, maybe the rest of eternity, then she pulled back, looking touched. "You're as bad as my father."

"How so?"

"Protective."

"Maybe." But he didn't want her returning to the basement without him. "Does Vince still live above the store?"

"Yeah. In the apartment upstairs."

"Promise me you won't go there without me."

"Ah," she whispered. "Now we're making promises."

Recalling how frightened she looked last night, he flexed his fingers, drawing her closer into an enveloping embrace. "This one, anyway."

"Vince couldn't be involved," she argued. "I've known him all my life."

He hedged. Vince Gato was an old family friend of the DiDolches. The relationship had never seemed close—it was more of an acquaintanceship—but still… "Honestly," he said, "the guy gives me the creeps."

She chuckled in disbelief. "Vince?"

"Not in a big way," he admitted. But there was something about the man he'd never liked, an undercurrent of violence or fear, maybe. Just something that bothered his sixth sense. "Look. Just promise me you won't go until this evening, when I can come with you."

"But what if Vince is home then?"

"If he's in his apartment, that's two stories above the basement. He won't hear us. Besides, he'll be in the shop during the day."

He didn't much like her expression. The vague disappointment and distracted quality added up to the fact that she hadn't heard him. It was pretty clear that she'd do whatever she pleased. She usually did. And usually, it was something he liked about her. Easily pliable women weren't his cup of tea.

"Okay," she finally said. "I'll wait."

"You're lying."

"You caught me."

He tightened his arms around her waist again. "I mean it, Carla. Don't."

Naked emotion suddenly showed in her eyes. The irises looked shiny, and her lips downturned slightly, making her look uncharacteristically pensive. This was the same dark look she got when her nightmares were plaguing her. "I'm beginning to think you care about me," she murmured, bringing her hand to his face.

Inwardly, he cursed, wishing she hadn't touched him so intimately. The moment became too raw, too telling. As if she'd touched his heart instead of his cheek. "Carla..."

All at once, the whole room seemed hushed. Suddenly, he realized he'd heard sounds before this: birds singing, traffic on Liberty Avenue, the slam of a door as the DiDolches headed downstairs to the café. Now, the strange silence carried only the soft exertion of their shared breath. The finger resting on his cheek rubbed downward until her thumb settled on his lower lip.

"Do you care about me, Tobias?"

Of course he did. "How could I not?"

But she was asking if he could love her again. When she didn't get the answer she'd wanted, she pushed her thumb between his lips and he felt powerless but to part his teeth, scraping them across her skin. Her eyes never leaving his, she used the thumb to explore his mouth in a way her tongue never could...touching the inner rims of his teeth, his gums, the roof of his mouth, until another wave of heat flooded straight to his groin.

Reaching, he closed his hand over hers, pulling her thumb just a fraction away, just far enough that he could speak. Huskily, he said, "I'll always care about you, Carla."

Her expression hardened, her eyes suddenly flashing, and for a brief moment, she looked like a petulant child. The look was gone in an instant, but he'd seen it before. It was the Italian spitfire in her. As if to punish him, she pushed her thumb inside his mouth once more, probing the depths as she rolled her hips against his. He sucked a breath through his clenched teeth as she inched upward, gasping as her heat found his heat.

If he'd forgotten how good they were together, he sure remembered now, but he wanted to defend his point of view. "You left me at the altar."

He could see her throat working as she swallowed. "You married Sandy Craig."

"Unfair," he countered. But suddenly, it didn't

seem to matter much. The most intimate part of her body was teasing him, and he was engorged with unrelieved want.

"I'm sorry," she whispered.

She was very aroused, too, and the moment was simply too much for him. Arms that had loosened around her waist now tightened in a claiming. Her breasts cushioned against him, leaving no room, and their eyes locked. Conflicting emotions coursed between them as if their bodies no longer existed, just their feelings.

And then their bodies seemed to return. Pushing a hand upward on her neck, under her hair, he scraped his nails over her scalp. He brought her nearer, not stopping until her mouth was an inch away, their breaths mingling. "Why did you run, Carla?"

Her voice was almost inaudible. "I don't know. Not really. I guess it was the nightmares. I told you that years ago. I know it's no excuse, but..."

What began as a punishing kiss ended in an explosion of fire, and he damned himself for not maintaining better boundaries. He simply couldn't. She tasted too good. He'd missed her too much. The mouth he plundered was like none he'd ever imagined. He wanted to take her, ravish her, brand her. He didn't want to stop until they were both reduced to smoldering, smoking ash. Somehow, he managed to break away, even though he thought he'd die from wanting to be inside her.

Her mouth was slack. "I don't know," she whispered again, now sounding helpless. "Why did you marry Sandy? Was it to hurt me?"

"Is that what you think?" He hated her for it—what

an ego! Then he marveled at himself. How could one woman fill him with so many contradictory feelings? "I wanted to get on with my life." Why couldn't she understand?

He should have known the question was coming. She was never going to stop asking until she got the answer she wanted. "Did you love her?"

He hesitated. Her eyes were so penetrating that they finally pulled the truth from him. Maybe the heat of her body helped. "Not the way I did you, Carla." Before she could ask anything more, he pressed a finger to her lips. "Now, stop," he added in a hushed whisper.

"I have to know what we're doing here, Tobias."

Right then, he became conscious of her heart. It was beating against his chest. He felt so close to her that, for a disjointed second, it seemed to be beating inside him. Exhaling another long stream of air, he tried to get his bearings. It didn't help. He was still in Carla's bed. No compass could help him find his way out of it. She was like a cottage that a kid's bread crumbs kept leading him back to. "I'm not going to let you leave me again," he finally said.

That was all he knew, all he could tell her. Suddenly, his voice broke, his fired-up body awash in a renewed wave of heat as his hands slid down her back, urging her to climb astride him and ride. "You broke my heart, Carla."

She could break his body, too. No woman should have this kind of power over a man. Maybe he should have walked out the back door when she'd come waltzing into the clinic. But now it was too late. Sliding a hand between them, she closed her fingers over his shaft. "I'm sorry," she said so softly that he barely heard.

But her apology could never be enough for the dark nights that had followed his wedding day. He'd never known how he'd borne the condolences. He'd hated how people at work, all of whom had been guests, had tiptoed around him. Never before nor since had Tobias Free been the object of anybody's pity. He never meant to be again. Call it false pride, but he wouldn't set himself up for it. Or would he? Right about now, with Carla on top of him, he felt as helpless as he had that day. "I don't know what we're doing, Carla," he whispered.

"I want us to be together," she whispered back.

He couldn't make promises. "That was up to you. You're the one who ran."

"Maybe I wouldn't now."

Hadn't he known that's what she'd wanted to say? The fingers he'd threaded through her hair tightened, and he shuddered against the unbearable softness of the strands. "Maybe isn't good enough."

"I know," she said.

Shutting his eyes, he felt her knees bracket his hips—and then all his thoughts were lost. They vanished abruptly, like a light going out. Trailers were left behind, the way smoke lingered after a candle was extinguished. Or the way whitecaps frothed as a boat churned through water. Love was left in the wake. Desire. Need. She'd set him on edge, left his body hot, his heart squeezing with emotion. Damn, he thought. Carla had done such a number on him.

Sensation took over as she crouched above him, lowering her mouth to his for a kiss that was too heartfelt, too hot.

"Even if it doesn't mean anything," she whispered, briefly lifting her lips from his, "I want to keep making love to you, Tobias."

God, he hated her for doing this to him. Lifting his chin, he found her mouth another time, drinking her in, plunging his tongue as he arched his hips, letting her know his lower body was ready to plunge, too. "It always means something, Carla. You know that."

That was the best he could offer. Maybe it was enough since, a blessed moment later, she lowered herself onto him. He'd never felt anything like it. She was dripping wet. So slick he could only gasp. Velvet heat closed over the head of his penis as her mouth descended, covering his in a determined kiss. She moved down…down…down, and as she overtook each inch, he twisted to capture every drop of her moisture.

"Ah…" He whispered as she took more control, her movements quicker, her hips rocking. "Ah…"

He was anxious to touch each inch of her—her skin that was growing damper with perspiration, the tips of breasts that he plucked excitedly until she whimpered in need, the inward dip of her waist that he caught his hands on. When she went over the edge, her body milked him, squeezing him until he knew he'd burst from the pleasure of it. But he didn't. He hung on to his control until she crested again. He was about to come when he heard her soft whisper right beside his ear. "It does mean something, doesn't it, Tobias?" she urged on a pant.

She'd caught him at the weakest moment. And as he lost control, he came, saying, "Damn you, Carla, you know I'm still in love with you."

11

HE LOVES ME.

All morning, as Carla worked with her parents in the café, the thought had run like an undercurrent beneath all her others. Whether she was arranging pastries in the display cases, or chatting with customers, or fixing espressos—she would hear Tobias's voice saying, "You know I'm still in love with you."

She had known it, of course. A man's body didn't lie. How Tobias made love to her spoke volumes. Still, she'd needed to hear it, and to know he hadn't loved Sandy in the same way. He loves me, she thought again. Which was why she had to do everything she could to remember…

It was the only way she could get him back. And yet, he'd been so worried about her exploring the passageway on her own. Guilt infused her as she stepped inside her bedroom closet and pulled away the panel. Her hand stilled on the wood, indecisively, but then she set it aside and dusted off her hands on her jeans skirt, sighing as the movement made her halter top come untucked. Just a moment ago, as she'd been serving lunch-time customers, she'd seen Vince leave his import business. No doubt, his employee, a twenty-year-old named Jim, was upstairs minding the shop. Even if Jim heard something downstairs, he wouldn't leave the counter to investigate. He'd just think the sounds were coming from next door.

"Which means the coast is clear," Carla murmured, taking a deep bracing breath, flicking on the flashlight and crouching down as she entered the claustrophobic space, reminding herself that there was nothing here except cobwebs. She needed to look around, to see if...

If she had any new memories. Quickening her pace, she was relieved when the passageway widened and she hit the staircase. "Easy," she whispered, standing upright. She could hear muted voices coming through the walls, first from the jewelry shop, then from the movie theater. The sounds were comforting, too, at least until they stopped.

Her steps stilled then. She was beside a storefront that was for rent. "Not to worry," she whispered, tamping down her feelings of unease and glancing around to calm herself. She couldn't see much. Despite the soaring temperatures outside, it was cool in the tunnel. Her chin lifted abruptly. Had she heard something? Shining the light toward the floorboards, she caught a movement. Feet scurried, and she fought the urge to scream.

"A mouse," she whispered shakily as the thankfully small rodent dived through a hole gnawed in the stairs.

She'd known they were here. Shaking her head as if to clear it of confusion, she continued down the tunnel, darkness surrounding her like a blanket as she moved. The splintered stairs creaked as she continued her descent. She couldn't see very far ahead, but the Gatos' basement had to be nearby, didn't it?

"How much farther?" Her voice was now tremulous, as weak as the beam of light she was using to guide her. With every step she took, something inside her soul seemed to weaken, too. It was the strangest, most inexplicable sensation. Just a few more steps, she thought. You're almost there, Carla.

But she didn't make it before the sensations that haunted her crowded into her mind, pushing everything else out. Images came from where they were hidden in her unconscious, rising like smoke and overtaking her, just like the nightmares she'd come to dread. The wavering light seemed to dim, and the silence seemed total. All-encompassing. Complete.

"Stay calm," she whispered, hating that she couldn't control herself better, or fight her fear. She felt like such a fool. But the past and present seemed to be fusing. It was as if she'd entered some weird time warp. Hadn't physicists explained things such as this? Wasn't there some intellectual theory about moments when the past and present really did overlap? Tobias would know....

She suddenly wished he was here with her right now, holding her hand as he had last night. She wished he was with her every night, too, always sleeping beside her, prepared to hold her during her nightmares, just as he had years ago. Staring over her shoulder, she considered going back. Yes, she could turn tail and run, but she could see nothing behind her, only the first few stairs in the weak beam of the flashlight. After that, there was only endless darkness.

Panic claimed her. Vaguely, she was aware that her grip tightened around the flashlight and that her knuckles ached because of it; her feet were frozen to the spot. When she tried to move forward, she couldn't. "Carla," she whispered, her voice eerily disembodied. This is just a staircase, nothing more.

But it was so dark. She inched another step downward, then another. It was as if an invisible hand had reached out to stop her, as if someone knew she was about to find something she shouldn't. Something hidden down here...

If she ran, she could be in the café with her parents within minutes, she reminded herself. She was being ridiculous. And yet, the past and present did seem to be coming together. There were her nightmares, then this moment. Her past with Tobias, and her present with Tobias...

The fear remained palpable. She concentrated on the descending stairs, ignoring the pitch darkness—until she startled again and whirled. Was it another mouse? Coming to a halt, she realized she must have spun in circles years ago. That's why the stairs appeared to be everywhere.

"Yes..."

She'd been sleepwalking. She'd awakened. Terror had overtaken her and she'd whirled, trying to run, but when she'd turned sideways, she'd thought the stairs were horizontal, not vertical...

"You're awake," she reminded herself, sliding a palm along her thigh as if that might orient her to the present.

And then she kept moving, tired of letting her imagination rule her life. If not for her dreams, she'd have married Tobias. Something salty stung her eyes—maybe dust, maybe tears. She had to conquer these demons. Wouldn't she do anything to have Tobias in her bed every night?

Even face these nightmares? "Here," she murmured in relief as her shaking hand traced the door to the Gatos' basement. As she pushed it open, she edged from behind the furnace and glanced around. Where to start?

No images appeared to guide her as she stepped farther into the room. Methodically, she began walking it like a circular grid, starting around the walls, then narrowing the circle with each pass. She stared at the ceiling. The floor. Her piercing eyes missing nothing, she studied the scarred surface of the desk that had haunted her dreams as minutes ticked by.

"Nothing," she whispered in disappointment, sharpening her gaze, taking in every object she could find—old wine kegs, racks of bottles, buckets and cleaning supplies. Did she really think she'd find something that would end her nightmares? Something that would bring her and Tobias together for good?

Suddenly, her eyes narrowed. She lurched forward. In a flash, she was kneeling. Scratch marks were around the wood of the flooring. One of the boards had been removed many times. But by whom? Vince Gato? Someone else? Her heart leaped into her throat, pounding not with fear now, but with excitement. Pivoting, she moved her eyes around the room, looking for a tool.

"There's a screwdriver." Rising just long enough to retrieve it from a shelf, she wedged the flat end between the boards. Wood cracked. Having been lifted out many times, the board gave easily. She set it aside, then peered into a hole less than a foot deep, scarcely deep enough for a man's hand.

Gold glinted from the dirt.

"Bingo," she whispered, feeling stunned and wishing Tobias was here to share this. The chastity belt. It was right here. With a sharp breath, she curled her fingers around the cold metal and lifted it out. Adrenaline was making her dry mouth taste acrid, but she barely noticed. The belt was heavier than she'd have expected, and the back was just exactly as it had appeared in the picture and her nightmares—gold circles meant to lock up a woman's body so it wouldn't know the pleasure of a man...

"Unbelievable," she whispered, realizing it was unlocked. Reaching into the hole once more, she lifted out an old, rusty key that looked nothing like those made in modern times. Her voice was hushed. "It looks about a million years old."

And the belt...

As she turned it in her hands, much like the man in her nightmares, she gasped. Even under the dim light, what she saw was enough to clarify why Gambolini had probably been murdered. Gems encrusted the front piece. A woman's pelvis would be covered in a waterfall-cascade of diamonds, emeralds and rubies. Glittering, they dazzled her eyes, sparkling as if from under a thousand suns.

"It has to be priceless," she managed to whisper.

Like many people before her over the centuries, she could only gape, her jaw slackening, her eyes unblinking. Museums had treasures worth less; she was sure of it. As she trailed her eyes down the sharply cut stones, she inhaled sharply. Quickly craning her head, she lifted her chin and stared toward the stairs that led into the import business.

Footsteps!

Yes, they'd sounded from above! She had to get out of here! Someone was coming! Instinctively, she scurried toward the furnace, then realized the belt and key were still in her hands. She had to put them back! Was there time? Or should she leave? Take the belt to the police?

It was definitely stolen, and it probably had something to do with an old, unsolved murder. She tugged the door panel. But it wouldn't open! It was stuck! Her heart hammering, she moved toward the hole in the floor again. Maybe if she put the belt in its hiding place, she could make up some excuse when the person came downstairs…

Her hand suddenly shook. The key dropped, clanking. Had the person upstairs heard? Pressing her lips together, she managed not to make a sound. Quickly, she leaned to retrieve the key, then realized the source of the clanking sound. The key had fallen through a metal grate. Dammit, she'd been standing over a vent.

Her trembling fingers thrust inside, but she couldn't reach the key. It was only an inch away, if that. She wiggled her fingers wildly, but still couldn't reach. Giving up, she curled her fingers around the edge of the grate and tugged. It wouldn't come up!

Upstairs, the door opened. Whoever it was, was coming downstairs now. Maybe it wasn't Vince. Maybe it was Jim. Maybe she could make up some kind of story…

Not knowing what else to do, she slid open the belt's waistband. Lifting her skirt, she stepped into the belt, shoving her legs through the leg bands. She stared toward the stairs. The door was ajar. Whoever opened it had changed his mind and gone back into the import businesses showroom.

She tugged at the metal surrounding her waist. Unsure how the belt functioned, she prodded the metal, sliding the waistband, inhaling sharply as it clicked. "Great." She tugged. But now it wouldn't budge.

She gave another tug. Another. But she was locked into a centuries-old chastity belt. "What a day," she whispered.

Racing forward, she covered the exposed hole in the floorboards as the upstairs door opened wider. She jerked her head toward the sound. Feet appeared first as the man came downstairs, then legs, then relief flooded her.

It wasn't Vince.

"Jim," she managed, hoping he didn't notice how her voice shook. Fortunately, he wasn't the brightest bulb in the ceiling. Her senses were heightened, her focus hyper-alert. She noticed every detail of his rectangular face, the short dark hair, the round dark eyes.

"Carla," he said in surprise, squinting as he hit the last stair. "How'd you get in here?"

She managed an innocent glance, even though she was still breathless, her heart pounding. "Didn't you see me? I walked right past you. The other night, Vince came over for dinner, and he promised my dad—" she reached into a dusty rack "—a bottle of this...uh..." She glanced down, her eyes scanning the label. "Burgundy. He said '65 was a great year. That Dad had to try it."

Jim didn't look suspicious. "Good," he said distractedly, heading for a shelf and lifting another bottle, "I'd talk to you," he apologized, "but I've got a customer. And Vince is—" The sound of footsteps upstairs cut him off. "Oh, I guess he's back."

Carla's heart thudded. "Uh...right."

"Jim?" Vince's voice sounded. "Are you down there?"

"Coming right up, boss."

Carla held her breath, hardly relieved when Jim bounded back up the steps. What if he told Vince she'd come for wine that Vince had never really promised her father? And how was she supposed to get out of the basement now? Edging forward, she stared at the floorboard, knowing it was only a matter of time before the missing belt was discovered. At least Jim hadn't noticed anything amiss....

Whatever was wrong here, the culprit had to be Vince. She doubted he had any legal right to the artifact, not given the way he'd hidden it. Content with how the board looked, she headed toward the access panel again, this time, taking the screwdriver with her. Inserting the edge into a crevice, she pried the door outward. Just as it swung open, she gasped, then whispered, "Tobias!"

Standing inside, he looked like a very tall, handsome sexy ghost. "Your parents said you were in the apartment," he said, his tone hushed as her eyes took in the tight white T-shirt molding his chest, then the well-worn jeans. "When I went into your room, I saw—"

Something in her eyes stopped him. "We have to get out of here."

"That's why I came," he whispered back. As she

slipped inside the passageway with him and pulled the door shut behind her, she heard Jim's voice sound again. "If you want to mind the shop," he called, apparently talking to Vince, "I'll check the stock in the basement."

Great. That meant she couldn't have Tobias help her lift the grate and get the key. Tobias was taking the flashlight and leading the way. "This morning, at the clinic," he began in a hushed tone, "I pulled Margaret Craig aside and got her to tell me more about Cornelius Sloane's porn collection."

Despite the circumstances, Carla felt jealousy twist inside her at the mention of Sandy Craig's mother. Pushing it aside, she said, "I found the belt."

As they hurried along, he said, "You what?"

"I'm wearing it," she explained urgently. When he whirled to face her, she pushed him forward. "C'mon," she said, keeping her voice low. "We have to get out of here! I dropped the key into a grate and..."

Fortunately, he kept moving. "You're wearing it?"

"Yes. I found it in the Gatos' basement." Quickly, she filled him in on the details.

"This morning," he began again, "I talked to Margaret. She'd been going through some of the old papers in the secret room at the Sloane mansion. And you'll never believe what she found."

Carla could barely believe any of this was happening. As the staircase ended, she and Tobias both ducked, entering into the narrower space. Relief flooded her when she saw the light from her bedroom. "What?"

"It turns out there's a bill of sale for the chastity

belt. I came over to tell you. It was imported by a seller in Rome and sold to Cornelius Sloane. He'd already paid for it. Which means Gambolini was probably appraising it for him..."

"When he was murdered," she finished.

Tobias nodded as he stepped into her closet, then reached back, offering a hand to help pull her out. "We need to get to the police."

She rose, squaring her shoulders as she moved out of the closet, into her room. Suddenly, she brought her hand to her mouth. "We can't go to the police."

Tobias raised an eyebrow. "Why not?"

She grabbed his hand and tugged him toward the front door of the apartment, hoping that whoever had hidden the chastity belt wouldn't discover it was missing anytime soon. "We can't go to the police," she repeated, feeling mortified at the thought. As they entered the living room, she continued. "I mean, I can't go there when I'm wearing..." At a loss and knowing time was of the essence, Carla merely glanced around the living room, then quickly lifted her skirt to expose her backside.

A wolf whistle sounded from behind her. "Wow."

"You don't know the half of it," she returned. "Literally."

"Meaning?"

Pausing just as they reached the door that led to the café, she hiked her skirt higher and turned around. "Take a look."

Each of his features froze into place. His brown eyes widened. His lips parted in shock. His shaggy blond eyebrows raised in high arches. And it looked as if he might remain just as he was until the end of time. Slowly, his features warmed and came to life again. His gaze moved over the front of the chastity belt. His hand followed, his long fingers tracing the gleaming gems as they caught the sunlight streaming through the windows. Clearly, not even touch convinced him this was real. "I can't believe it."

"Believe it," she said.

He whistled again. "I was right," he managed. "It looks great on you." His attempt to joke fell flat. Finally, he added, "It must be worth a fortune."

She nodded. "The watercolor at the Sloane mansion only showed the back. I don't know why."

"Maybe there's another companion picture somewhere, showing the front."

"Maybe." But the point was, she didn't want to be responsible for wearing something priceless. "I have to get out of it. And it's locked."

"Locked?" Despite the circumstances, he looked very sorry when she dropped her skirt. "Well, when we get to the police..." he began.

She could only shake her head as she urged him downstairs. "No way," she whispered. "I don't want a bunch of cops standing around, gawking at me."

Tobias's eyes narrowed as if to say he didn't like the idea any more than she did, if for different reasons. "But what are we going to do..."

"C'mon," she said again, pushing through the door into the café. She gave her mother and Jenna a jaunty wave as she continued pulling Tobias forward, winding around tables and customers as she moved toward the outer door.

"Aren't you two going to sit down?" Mary called, her dark eyebrows raised in surprise.

''Tobias and I need to talk,'' Carla said in her best woman-to-woman voice.

At that, Mary gave a satisfied nod as if to say she understood perfectly. Which, of course, she didn't.

''Where are we going?'' Tobias asked again.

Carla cast a glance toward Gato and Gambolini's as they stepped onto the hot sidewalk and into the warm summer sunlight. Once more, she hoped Vince wasn't involved in this, and that there was some reasonable explanation as to why a priceless artifact was buried in his basement.

And then, knowing she desperately needed a locksmith, she said, ''To my cousin, Carmine's.''

12

"LEAN FORWARD and put your hands on the worktable," Tobias murmured. As his eyes trailed lovingly over her backside, Carla's skin tingled. Astonishing, she thought. Nothing more than a look—and Tobias could make all her nerve endings unravel like ribbons. His words were even sexier. "And hike your skirt higher, Carla."

Despite the adventures of the past hour, she couldn't help but shoot him a saucy smile over her shoulder. "Little good it will do you, Tobe. I'm rather inaccessible at the moment."

"That you are."

Tossing Carmine's cell phone onto the table, she sighed. "As inseparable as he is from this thing, I wonder why he left it when he went out?" She'd just used the phone to call her mother, in case Carmine came into the café, which he did sometimes around lunchtime.

"I don't know," Tobias returned, his eyes still taking in her unusual attire. "But I'm kind of glad he's not in the shop."

She was, too. "Yeah. But like I said, it's doing you precious little good to have me alone."

"Joke's on you, sweetheart," said Tobias as he fished around, his hands skating over the items on one of Carmine's worktables. "Because I don't have the faintest idea how to pick a lock." He was staring into one of her cousin's toolboxes.

She shot him a droll glance. "What kind of man are you?"

Tobias leveled her a stare. "As soon as I get you out of those gold panties, I'll be glad to show you."

Wiggling her nose, she tried to ignore the scents, but it was impossible. Oily rags were strewn on benches, making the place looked and smell like a car garage. "In here?"

"Why not?"

"So romantic," she said dryly.

"Once I start kissing you," he promised, "you won't care."

There was probably a lot of truth in that. "That's something else I missed about you," she volleyed. "Your ego."

He laughed. "Other parts of my anatomy are even larger."

She groaned. Then she couldn't help it; she laughed, too. And it felt good. Otherwise, she had a belly full of butterflies. Hopefully, they'd be heading toward the police station in Oakland soon. But what if her actions were tantamount to turning Vince Gato in to the law? The thought made her jittery. She'd known the man ever since she was a little kid. Occasionally, he dined at her parents, too, as had his ancestors before him.

It was all so confusing. So was everything else about her life in the past few days. Tobias had reentered her world, and her mind felt strangely preoccupied, as if the last vestiges of her nightmares were about to give way. Maybe they'd break free, like a balloon cut from a bunch.

Shutting her eyes, she imagined her fingers uncurling from around the string of a bright yellow balloon, and then she watched it as it fishtailed into the air, rising higher, until it was lost to a blue sky and clouds. Then she swallowed hard, trying to tell herself not to hope too much. Unless she was absolutely sure she'd go through with a wedding, she had no right to be here with Tobias, not really. Oh, she wanted him sexually. Craved him like a thirsty woman in a desert, in fact. But she'd hurt him too much before. Now she knew she'd never do so again.

"What are you thinking?"

Thoughts too heavy for a moment that had turned strangely light and airy, despite the fact that they'd shortly be on their way to a precinct. She spoke her mind, anyway. "I don't know that we should be, uh, seeing each other again," she murmured. "I'm worried, Tobias."

He was at her side in a heartbeat, brushing a lock of hair from her temple with his fingertip. His eyes were unreadable, and she knew that, deep down, he was conflicted. Nevertheless, he said, "What brings this up?"

She shrugged. "I know you still love me," she whispered. "And I love you. But I don't want to hurt you."

He merely delivered a kiss, then returned to searching the worktable. "You won't hurt me," he murmured.

"You sound so sure." Much surer than he had this morning, when they'd made love.

There was an edge of steel in his voice. ''We're going to get to the bottom of this, Carla.''

It was what he'd often said in the past, but she felt a surge of hope, anyway. ''Sorry,'' she murmured, shaking her head as if to clear it of confusion. She reminded herself that her jumbled-up feelings were due to the mystery she'd gotten involved in, too. And then, of course, there was the fact that Tobias was only a foot away and her backside was thoroughly exposed. When memories of her nightmares intruded on her consciousness again—just an image of the scarred desk in the Gatos' basement, then the scary stairway with its horizontal steps—she pushed them away...

''Do you even know what a lock pick looks like?'' she asked, mustering a brighter tone, determined to restore the lighter mood she'd experienced just a moment before.

''Not really,'' he admitted.

As much as she wanted out of the chastity belt, she felt another smile tug her lips. Years ago, she'd been so lucky to find Tobias. He'd been so different from her family, and yet so able to fit into it. Despite his career in academic research and his decidedly WASP upbringing, there was something earthy about him to which the deepest core of her responded.

While she waited for him to find a tool he could use, she sighed, glancing around, her eyes trailing over dusty worktables, strewn with various locks, most of which were coated with grease. Mounted above her, on the wall, were pegboards from which keys were hanging, and through a doorway, she could see the storefront. Hopefully, no one would show up, wanting help at the counter. ''At least I had a key to get in,'' she offered conversationally. She always watered Carmine's plants when he went out of town.

Tobias was using an index finger to stir things in the toolbox, as if the right lock pick was cream that he could make rise to the surface. "We probably just missed him."

Carmine had left a note on the door, saying he'd be back soon. "Like you said, it's just as well that he's gone," she decided, crinkling her nose when she saw what looked to be the leftovers of a Chinese takeout lunch. Carmine wasn't exactly the world's best housekeeper.

Tobias lifted a thin piece of metal from the box, held it up and surveyed it. "Why's that?"

"On the drive over here," she began, "I realized I might not want my cousin undressing me any more than the police."

"But me," Tobias murmured, coming behind her and circling his arms around her waist, "you don't mind?"

"Nope."

Hugging her, he nuzzled past her hair, using his chin to push it from her neck. Settling his mouth on the exposed column, he looped wet kisses from her ear to her collarbone. Tilting her head farther back, she shut her eyes as his tongue swirled blissfully, then she shivered as he caught her earlobe between his teeth. For a moment, she forgot she'd been snooping around Vince Gato's basement just moments before, and that she was locked into a stolen, jewel-laden chastity belt.

Not that she really could forget, of course. The belt was heavy and uncomfortable. On the drive to Carmine's, she'd had to grit her teeth in order to bear how the metal encircling her waist was knocking against her hipbones. The leg bands chafed, and the jewel-encrusted crotch area was so heavy that her body weight actually felt displaced.

Now Tobias's tongue was making all those sensations vanish. A soft sigh was torn from between her lips as the tip of his tongue traced inside her ear. After exploring the inner rim, he licked deeper into the interior, then he blew on all the wet places.

"We have to get to the police," she murmured.

"Anxious to get out of this thing, huh?"

She nodded, wanting to make love.

He leaned away. "I'm glad you don't mind me undressing you," he said, his voice lowering seductively.

"It's nothing you haven't seen before."

"And hopefully will again," Tobias agreed dryly, his voice making her melt inside. Everything turned runny. Warmth was sliding through each inch of her as he drifted his gaze once more over the chastity belt. The thong panties she wore beneath were so scanty that they clearly didn't mar the visuals for him. He made a throaty sound. "I sure hope you don't have to go to the bathroom anytime soon."

Her lips quirked. "Glad to see you're enjoying my discomfort."

"I'm just curious as to how women survived in these things."

"Me, too. It's sort of like a bra. Just something else men invented to torture us."

He kissed her again. "Am I torturing you?"

She glanced pointedly around the workshop. "I'm

sure Carmine's got some thumb screws around here somewhere."

"No doubt. Maybe even nipple clips."

She wouldn't put it past her cousin. "Your mind," she offered in a chiding whisper. "How indelicate."

He shook his head. "Surely, in the old days, when women actually wore these things, someone other than her husband had to have a key."

Settling her hands around the edge of the worktable, Carla leaned farther over it, since Tobias was getting ready to start working on the lock. She shot him a long, sideways glance. "Yeah," she said. "The women."

Wheels spun noisily on the tile floor as he dragged a stool toward her, then seated himself so he could get to work. He glanced up. "You think the women had keys? Wouldn't that defeat the purpose?"

"Of course they had spare keys," she clarified, rolling her eyes. "That way, they could sleep with whoever they wanted while their husband was off, fighting wars."

"Whomever."

"Don't get nasty and correct my grammar just because you've realized women control their own sexual fate."

"No man would ever make that mistake with you, Carla."

Twisting her hips, she tried to see what Tobias was doing now, but she couldn't. Judging from the sound, he was inserting that long, skinny piece of metal into the keyhole. Once more, she wished she hadn't dropped the key into the grate as he wiggled the metal piece this way, then that. After a moment, he sighed in frustration.

"What?" she asked, feeling a first blush of alarm. "You can't open the lock?" Panic threatened. Was she really going to be stuck in this thing? Was she going to have to expose her hind end to the police or Carmine? What if she did have to go to the bathroom?

Tobias said, "Don't give up on me yet."

A slow smile curled the corners of her mouth. She didn't intend to—not now, not ever. For another long moment, she kept her eyes trained over her shoulder, taking in the blond top of his head, able to catch glimpses of eyes he'd narrowed in concentration. Scooting closer, he slid his thighs on either side of hers, bracing himself against her body as he worked, the feel of his well-muscled legs as arousing as his kisses. She shivered.

And this time, it wasn't from fear. She could barely believe she'd been creeping around Vince Gato's basement less than an hour ago, scared spitless. "So, Margaret has a bill of sale, proving the chastity belt belonged to Cornelius Sloane?" she prompted as Tobias splayed his fingers and settled them on her waist to steady her.

"Yeah," he muttered, concentrating on the lock.

"I'd hate to be stuck in a chastity belt forever," she suddenly said nervously.

"Me, too."

"You're not wearing it."

He sighed. "I mean I want you out of it."

"Any reason?"

"Purely selfish," he answered. "I want sex."

Edging backward a fraction, she settled more firmly

between his spread legs, and when her backside met his groin, she sucked in a breath. ''Hold still,'' he murmured distractedly, flexing his fingers on her hip to keep her in place as he continued working.

''Am I destroying your focus?''

''Yes.''

Her smile broadening, she couldn't help but have a little fun. Shimmying, she lifted her skirt a higher, then whispered, ''Hurry, Tobias.''

''I'm trying.''

Her eyes locked on his. ''You'd better. I'm getting wet.''

He didn't bother to say another word, just lowered his head and began working in earnest. After a moment, he said, ''You sure do know how to motivate a man.''

''I haven't even begun,'' she promised.

A click sounded. And he sent her a dazzling smile. ''Now you can.''

She watched as he rose to his feet and kicked back the stool, sending it across the room on its rollers. Taking her by the shoulders, he simply turned her around to face him. Before her skirt could fall back down, he grabbed the hem and kept it raised, pressing the fabric into her hand.

And then he simply stared at her, wearing the belt. His eyes glazed, and she figured it wasn't just from the fact that diamonds and rubies encased her pubic area. His lips parted, and he exhaled a shaky sigh as he cupped his hand over the gems, then his caress followed the contours of the metal, until he was gliding his hands around her waist. As he unsnapped the back, he said, "We don't have to go straight to the police, do we, Carla?"

Slowly, she shook her head. "I think we can spare a minute, Tobias." Gingerly, hoping not to further hurt herself, she slid the chastity belt downward on her thighs, then stepped out of it. The thong she wore beneath quickly followed.

"Oh, no," he murmured, his sigh ragged, his hands bracketing her waist.

She glanced down as his thumbs rubbed gentle circles into her skin. Everything he touched heated up immediately. She squinted. "What?"

"You're bruised."

He was right. Dark-gray and purplish places were rising on her skin where the heavy metal had chafed her. "You could kiss it and make it feel better."

Leaning, he did just that, pressing his cool mouth to where the metal had clanged and burned. Arching, she threaded her hands into his hair, guiding his mouth, urging it lower. Just hearing the need in his voice made her gush. "Is that all you want me to kiss, Carla?"

She hazarded another quick glance at the plate glass window in the next room, then the doorway. In addition to Carmine's note, which was scrawled with a Sharpie pen in something that barely resembled the English language, there was also a sign on the door with a clock timer. The long black hands had been positioned at seven. As if Carmine had ever awakened at such an hour in his life. She just hoped he didn't decide to come back anytime soon.

"I can think of a few other places where I'd like to feel your mouth," she admitted.

"Why don't you tell me?" Tobias whispered back.

And so she did, naming each place for him, one by one.

LESS THAN AN HOUR AGO, when he'd returned from his errands, Vince had known something was wrong. He'd felt it in his bones, hadn't he? Now his grip tightened on the steering wheel of his gray Oldsmobile. Hunching his shoulders, he peered through the windshield, looking for Carla's car. It was a white Honda Accord.

No matter how hard he tried, he couldn't tamp down the anger boiling within him. It was bubbling to the surface, feeling dangerous. How dare she steal the belt? And why hadn't he been able to stop her? He'd been in the shop awhile before that fool, Jim, had come back up from the basement and mentioned that Carla was downstairs. He'd said Carla had come for the wine he'd promised her father.

But Vince hadn't promised Larry a bottle. Vince had run downstairs, and the second he'd entered the basement he'd known his heirloom was gone. His treasure! The Gato legacy! He meant to bequeath it to his sons! It hardly mattered that his ancestor had stolen it, even killed for it. All that mattered was that the belt was gone!

He'd rushed to the floorboard, realizing she'd pried it loose. She'd taken the key, too. He'd gnashed his teeth. After all these years, little Carla had remembered the horrible night when she'd found the hidden stairway.

He'd been seated at the desk, admiring his treasure, when he'd sensed a presence behind him. Turning and staring into the darkness, he'd seen three-year-old Carla, her eyes wide, blank and unseeing. In her long white nightgown, she'd looked like a ghost.

He'd said something to her…something nasty. He couldn't remember what now. Why would he—after all these years? The whole thing happened so long ago. Right after he'd spoken, she'd dropped into a faint. That had scared him. She was only three and as light as a feather, but when she'd thudded to the floor, she'd hit so hard that he'd thought she was dead.

She was breathing, though. Panicking, he'd carried her back through the tunnel, to her bedroom, hoping she'd been sleepwalking, the way her parents said she did. Slipping her between her sheets, he'd covered her, then crept from the room again, shutting the door to the staircase, hoping she'd never find it again.

And what if she did? he'd thought at the time. She was just a little girl; it would be her word against his. And then later, he'd known he was safe because the DiDolches told him about Carla's silly dreams. Oh, how they'd laughed when they'd talked about the golden underwear.

"Golden underwear," Mary DiDolche had said so many times, chuckling. "Can you believe how kids' minds work?"

But now, after all these years, Carla had come to take Vince's treasure. "That sly little…"

He tried to keep his eyes on traffic and his foot off the gas pedal. He wanted to race to Carmine's shop, but the last thing he needed was to get a ticket.

Still, he had to reach Carla. What if she was going to the police? His throat went dry as he patted the gun he'd stuffed into his waistband. He'd never used it before, never had occasion to. He'd kept it for years, shoved under the counter in the store, in case he was ever robbed.

"Almost there," he whispered, mentally willing the traffic on Fifth Avenue to go faster.

He'd been in the café, moments ago, when Carla called to ask her mother if she'd seen Carmine.

"She's having problems with her car lock," Mary had announced conversationally.

"Yeah, right," muttered Vince now. Somehow, Carla had managed to lose the key and get herself locked into his priceless treasure. "A treasure I want back," he whispered.

13

''WE'RE GOING to the station in Oakland, right?'' Carla squinted as she guided the Accord through Fifth Avenue traffic, toward mansion row and the dream clinic. Directly overhead, the bright white noontime sun was shining down, its rays bouncing off every surface, from the clean, polished white hood of her car to the chrome on the bumper of the lime-green Miata in front of her.

''It's the closest precinct,'' answered Tobias.

''We could stop at the clinic,'' she suggested, brushing her frizzing hair back from her face to relieve herself of the day's heat. ''And put the belt into the safe.''

Tobias shook his head. ''No. We might as well go straight to the station and let them deal with it.''

She nodded. The sooner the artifact was out of their hands, the better. She hardly wanted to be responsible for something that had to be worth a king's ransom. Shifting in the seat, she scooted closer to the wheel, then she fumbled above her, checking the visor to see if her sunglasses were there. They weren't. ''Drats,'' she muttered.

''What?''

''My sunglasses,'' she explained, hazarding a glance beside her, where the chastity belt rested between her and Tobias. Even inside the car, the sun's piercing rays had found it, making the gems gleam. She recalled the quick, hot lovemaking inside Carmine's shop, then forced her attention onto the road again.

"It *is* sunny out," Tobias murmured.

"And hot." The air was moist and muggy. Despite the bright sun, storm clouds were starting to gather in the far distance, ready to roll in with another summer storm. Hearing a horn behind her, Carla glanced into the rearview mirror and gasped, seeing a gray Oldsmobile. Instinctively, she tightened her fingers over the wheel, turning her knuckles white. "It's Vince," she said. "He's right behind us."

Tobias glanced over his shoulder, through the back windshield and cursed softly. "He's waving at us to pull over."

"Should I?" Keeping one hand on the wheel, she dug into the pocket of her jeans skirt as she shifted into the other lane, hoping to put a car between her and Vince.

"No. Keep going."

Tamping down her emotions, she tried to stay calm, but her voice hitched with fear. "You're sure?"

"Yeah."

Vince had shifted lanes. He was behind them again. Swerving, she returned to the lane where she'd been previously, pulling her car behind the Miata, but once more Vince followed suit. Which meant he definitely had something to do with this. He'd known the belt was hidden in his basement all this time...all these years. A voice played in her mind, saying, *ever since you were a little kid.* But was Vince the man she'd seen? She didn't think so, but…

Suddenly, the sunlight seemed too bright. She blinked, but it glanced off the hood just as a sunspot burst in the rearview mirror, blinding her. Lifting her chin, she shook her head like an animal throwing off water.

Tobias looked at her, concerned. "What?"

"Nothing," she said, realizing her hand had stilled in the pocket of her jeans skirt. She'd brought along Carmine's cell phone, and now she pressed it into Tobias's hand. "Call nine-one-one."

As he did, she darted her eyes right, then left. Should she turn onto a side street, or stay on the main avenue? The traffic wasn't heavy, but she was hemmed in. Still, with so many people watching, what could Vince do?

"He's waving again," she said, watching him motion her to pull over, then half listening as Tobias spoke into the phone, informing the operator of their situation and location.

"We have a priceless artifact," he finished. "We're taking it to the nearest precinct in Oakland."

A motor roared. Then everything seemed to happen out of sequence. The phone flew from Tobias's hand as the Accord lurched forward. Metal crunched, and Carla's chest slammed the steering wheel. The seat belt pulled, the shoulder strap catching taut on her neck, strangling her, pushing panic through her. Vince had rammed them from behind!

Tobias grabbed her, pushing her back against the seat, but not before she'd instinctively hit the gas, desperate to escape. Just as she crashed into the Miata, she realized the mistake.

A horn sounded. Vince's? No...the Miata. In front of her, the green car swerved, pulling to the curb, the driver getting out of the way. A motor gunned—the Oldsmobile's, Carla realized. "He's going to hit us again," she gasped.

"Keep driving."

The next crash was more jarring. Her head whipped back at the impact. "I can't! He's going to hurt us."

Tobias was fishing on the floor for the phone. "Pull into the clinic."

"What?" She could barely think. All her senses had heightened, her eyes sharpening as they shifted between the windshield and mirror. Stepping on the gas, she tried to outdistance Vince. Cars were weaving to the sides now, parting as drivers realized the Oldsmobile was intentionally smashing into her.

"We'll put the belt in the safe, like you said." Lifting the phone to his ear once more, Tobias listened. "Yeah," he muttered. "We're still here...the guy's hitting us from behind now. We're going to the university's dream clinic." Tobias gave the address, then cursed softly, turning off the phone. He tossed it beside him, into a compartment between the seats.

Her eyes riveted on the gray car. "What did the operator say?"

"The cops are on their way."

"I hope they hurry," she said nervously.

He looked behind them again just as the Oldsmobile surged. Metal crumpled again. Glass shattered, probably the taillights. Tobias's arm flew out, and as his hand wrapped around the dashboard to steady himself,

Carla looked into the mirror again. What she saw of Vince Gato wasn't comforting. Thick, black unruly hair was thrust from the heavy man's face, and his eyes, even from this distance, looked menacing.

"There." Tobias pointed. "Pull into the driveway."

Her throat was raw with panic. "He's following us, Tobias."

"There's not much we can do."

He was right. The way Vince was crashing into them, they could be seriously hurt. "Okay."

"Park by the door. We'll run inside. We can lock him out, and put the belt inside the safe until the cops come."

Ahead, she could see the high wrought-iron gates of the Sloane mansion. As if rehearsing her next moves, she visualized the interior, the open gate, the circular driveway that looped around a fountain. She saw herself and Tobias racing inside, squealing to a stop before the front doors. Both car doors would swing open like wings, then she and Tobias would leap out.

But it didn't happen that way.

When she slowed to take the turn into the gate, Vince speeded, his left headlight taking off her fender. Dragging, the squealing chrome scraped the pavement, making sparks fly. Overcorrecting, she swerved and fishtailed, the steering wheel spinning from her hands. As Tobias grabbed it, Vince attacked once more, and the wheel wrenched to the right. The tires turned in the same direction, launching them off the roadway, onto the lawn.

Her fingers clung to the wheel. The terrain was bumpy, but she kept her hands steady. Braking slowly, trying to regain control, she realized they were driving over a flower bed. In the mirror, she saw that Vince had fallen back. He was still on the paved driveway. Good. There was some distance between them.

Looking through the windshield again, she saw a tree and hit the brakes. How had it gotten there? Right in front of her? Dammit, she'd braked too late. The tree met the hood, dead center, the impact throwing her and Tobias forward again.

The next thing she heard was his voice. "Run!"

Glancing beside her, staring in shock, she was barely able to realize they'd just wrecked. Tobias had slumped. His hand was trapped under the driver's seat! How had that happened? "What?" she managed, her racing mind still trying to comprehend what was happening.

"Run," he urged again, twisting his body to look at her. "I can handle this. Run before Vince gets here. Take the belt. Run inside, just like we planned."

She couldn't leave him here. But he'd never forgive her if she didn't try to get away. Releasing her seat belt, she reached down, trying to help him twist his wrist free. Obviously, he'd removed his seat belt too soon. When they'd hit the tree, he'd rolled under the dashboard.

Panicked, she glanced behind her as the driver's door of the Oldsmobile slowly opened.

Tobias's brown eyes lasered into hers. "Run!"

And she did.

Moved by something other than her own volition, she grabbed the phone and belt, then kicked open her door. She didn't feel the stifling August heat or the soft grass. She didn't hear Vince's footsteps pounding on the pavement as he gave chase, either. The whole world narrowed to the double front doors in front of her. She had to reach them! To get inside!

A shot rang out. A gunshot? Lord, did Vince really have a gun? Whirling, craning her head, she nearly lost her footing. Sliding in the grass, a sharp pain shot up her leg, coming from her ankle.

Then she saw Vince. Yes! He was behind her, waving a revolver.

From in front of her, another voice sounded. ''Oh my God!''

Shifting her focus to the doors again, Carla realized someone had come outside! Margaret Craig! Sandy's mother! Her heart hammered when Margaret ran back inside, slamming the door.

No doubt, she'd locked it to keep Vince out. Carla's feet were still moving. Her unconscious mind was leading her now. Her steps flew across a veranda, then into the grass again. The old well on the lawn, she thought.

Yes. She'd forgotten about it. She'd noticed it the night she and Tobias were walking in the garden. ''There it is!''

A moment later, she was crouched behind the circular stone structure. It rose about three feet from the ground, just high enough that she could hide behind it, protecting herself if Vince fired another bullet.

Her back against the stones, Carla sat on her haunches, suddenly aware of her body. Breath was coming in gulps, and her legs were weak, shaking. How had they supported her? Pain wracked her ankle. Her mouth and throat were painfully dry. Her tongue tasted like metal. Somehow, she turned and raised herself up, so she could look over the edge of the well. Vince was only twenty paces away. To her left, in the bushes, she saw a moving shadow and realized Tobias had gotten free and followed.

She blew out a shuddering breath. Vince was unaware of him....

"Hold it right there," she shouted, then licked her lips, willing moisture into her mouth.

When Vince only slowed to a walk, she raised the chastity belt over the opening of the well. Who knew how deep it was? If she dropped the belt, it might be lost forever. When she dangled it farther over the gaping hole, Vince stopped in his tracks. "I'll drop it," she warned.

He waved the gun. "Toss it to the side, Carla."

From the corner of her eye, she could see Tobias edging toward Vince. He was in the open now, moving silently over the grass, his arms held out to his sides, ready to tackle the other man. He was thirty feet from Vince, now twenty...

"Drop the gun," she managed. "Or I'll throw the belt into the well."

Vince froze. In fact, everything seemed to stop. The garden was shady, and despite the intense sunlight elsewhere on the lawn, Vince's face was thrown into shadow. Something about his expression bothered her, touching the deeper confines of her mind. She fought the feeling, trying to stay focused. Behind Vince and a few feet to his right, Tobias took another step forward.

It was the wrong time for the phone to ring.

Startled, she nearly lost her grip on the belt, then she realized the phone was in her other hand. Using her thumb, she pressed Talk. She kept her eyes locked on Vince, trying hard not to look at Tobias, not wanting Vince to follow her gaze and discover he was there. She barely recognized the scratchy sound of her own voice. "Hello?"

"Carla?"

It was her cousin. "Carmine," she whispered. "This really isn't a very good time." It was the world's greatest understatement.

Ignoring her, Carmine said, "Where are you? What's going on? Where's my phone?"

She should have known the man couldn't last long without his cell phone. But how did a woman explain circumstances such as this? That she was standing in the garden of the Sloane mansion, with Vince Gato pointing a gun at her, while a man she'd nearly married years ago crept up behind him, looking like something out of a men's action-adventure movie, and all while she was dangling a priceless artifact over a dry well, threatening to toss it down the hole…an artifact that she'd been locked into until only a few minutes ago? Right before she clicked the phone back off again, Carla settled on simply saying, "Sorry, but I'll have to get back to you on this, Carmine."

Setting the phone gingerly on the rim of the well, Carla rose another inch, peeking over the stones, hoping she could get Vince to drop the gun.

"I mean it, Vince!" she warned. As she waved the chastity belt above the opening, she realized it was her best weapon. The more she jiggled it, the more mesmerized Vince looked. The glitter of the cut gems danced in his dark eyes. No wonder he'd kept it buried in his basement. He was utterly entranced by it.

TOBIAS MOVED into a crouch, his knees flexed so he could lunge. He was maybe nine feet behind Vince now, then eight...

Suddenly, Vince whirled. As he wrenched to look behind him, his gun hand went wild. Tobias dove, capturing Vince's arm as it came down in an arc. Tobias forced it to rise again, so the weapon pointed skyward. Another shot sounded, the report deafening, the sparks visible as a bullet discharged. Carla's eyes shifted from one man to the other. They were locked in a death struggle! Tobias's hand wrapped around Vince's wrist, but Vince was fighting hard to keep control of the revolver.

Carla gasped. "Tobias!"

Her fingers lost their grip. The belt fell away. Vaguely, she was aware it had fallen into the well, that the gold was scraping the sides of a stone wall. But she was already running. "Tobias!"

She'd nearly reached him when he managed to wrestle the gun from Vince's grasp. Drawing back his long arm, Tobias came up swinging, releasing the weapon when his hand reached the apex. Barrel over grip, the gun spun through the air, too far away for Vince to retrieve it. Just as it landed in a bush, rustling down into the leaves, and just as Tobias finished subduing the other man, Vince slowly turned toward Carla.

Time stopped then.

There was something about his face...about the yellow cast of the summer sunlight streaming through the trees. In the garden's murky shadows, his chin lifted and as she took in the profile...

Images that had remained static in her mind for

years began snapping into place, coalescing to make sense. Each image seemed like a puzzle piece. She saw herself standing in the darkness, wearing a white nightgown. Then her hand was groping over a wall, searching for a light switch.

And then everything turned dark.

Déjà vu, she thought, her pulse racing. The world was folding in half. Past and present were overlapping. She was staring into impenetrable blackness, breathing stuffy air. She was scared and trapped, and all around her, stairs ran every which way. Some went upward. Some downward. Each time she whirled, they looked horizontal.

And now it all made sense.

While sleepwalking, she'd found the access panel and the hidden staircase, and she'd followed it down to the Gatos' basement. Vaguely, she remembered waking. She'd been trying to go to the bathroom, to get herself a glass of water, but instead she'd wound up in a dark, dingy room she'd never seen before. And that's when Mr. Gato slowly turned around. He'd been seated at a desk, staring at a pair of golden underwear...

The voice she'd heard in the far reaches of her consciousness now played again, saying, "If you marry, you will die." Except that now, it was Vince Gato's voice. And that wasn't what he'd said at all.

"Oh, no," she whispered. "'If you *tell Mary,* you will die,' was what he'd said. "Oh, my God." Carla's hand rose to cover her mouth. He'd threatened her, warning her not to tell her mother! He hadn't mentioned marriage at all! He'd said her mother's name.

"Mary," she whispered again. *If you tell Mary, you will die…*

Carla had been terrified. She remembered that now. She'd probably fainted. It was the only thing that made sense. Because for all these years, she'd been haunted by deeper, darker images, too. Ones she'd never mentioned to anyone. Or even acknowledged to herself….

As if from a drugged consciousness, thoughts began dragging upward through years of sleep, and she recalled being carried through a maze, back up the staircase, her white nightgown draped across her ankles. The only time the image had so much as teased her consciousness was in high school, when she and Tobias had seen the movie *Phantom of the Opera.* Now, she realized that seeing the movie had made her nightmares return.

"Carla?"

Ignoring Tobias, she stepped closer to stare at Vince. "You must have carried me back to my room that night," she whispered. "It was you. Why?" Her lips parted in astonishment. He knew her family; he'd dined at her house. With the realization, a tentacle of fear slid through her. If he hadn't been a family friend, maybe Vince Gato would have done far worse to her that night, in order to protect his stolen treasure.

His expression was thunderous. If Tobias wasn't so strong, Vince would make a run for it, but Tobias held him fast. "Why?" he growled. "You know why. The belt was our heirloom. Our heritage. The Gatos' future."

"The belt belonged to Cornelius Sloane," she countered.

"The Gatos!" he proclaimed, the name ringing out with pride.

"Your great-great grandfather's partner, Gambolini, appraised it for Cornelius Sloane," she ventured again, her eyes searching him, hoping to see some admission of his wrongdoing.

All she saw was craftiness, and the dark gleam of greed.

"Anthony got the belt for our family, Carla." As his eyes pierced hers, he muttered something in Italian she didn't understand.

Her heart hammered. Her gaze slid to Tobias's and comprehension passed between them. "Anthony Gato used the stairwell," she guessed, "to go into the basement and kill his partner when he was appraising the belt..."

Vince smiled. "My great-great grandfather had been dining at your apartment in fact."

Hearing it sparked anger in her Italian blood. Vaguely, she was aware that people from the clinic had come outside to watch the action, now that Vince was safely subdued, among them Sloane Junior and Margaret Craig. Carla said, "Your great-great grandfather was dining at our apartment the night he killed Gambolini? We were his alibi?"

"And well worth a priceless gem," Vince agreed.

"Maybe." Tobias spoke for the first time. "But you covered up a murder, Vince. And the belt isn't rightfully yours."

"You're going to pay for this," Vince Gato snarled.

"No," Carla returned, loving the taste of justice in her mouth almost as much as she enjoyed the renewed taste of love that Tobias had put there. "I think *you're* going to pay, Vince."

Right then, from far down Fifth Avenue, sirens sounded.

"'IF YOU TELL MARY, you will die,' Tobias whispered many hours later, when Carla was in his bed, curled in his arms. It had been a long day, much of it spent with the police, who'd retrieved the chastity belt from the well with all its precious stones intact. Reporters had arrived, too, when they'd gotten tips about the dramatic resolution to a century-old murder. And then Tobias had to deal with Sloane Junior, who'd been so astonished to find himself the proud rightful owner of a priceless artifact that he'd changed his mind again and offered Tobias, not Margaret Craig, the lease to the mansion. While Tobias was glad, losing the lease had made him realize that he'd wanted a more modern, efficient work space, anyway, if he could get it. And Carla was trying to convince him he could. Besides, Cornelius Sloane's collection did deserve to be displayed.

Dinner with their parents hadn't been much easier. The Frees were horrified at the danger he and Carla had been in. And the DiDolche's were beside themselves. No matter how Carla had tried to convince them otherwise, they blamed themselves for not understanding the root of her nightmares. Vince Gato, while not a close friend, had been a guest in their home. Because they'd trusted him, they were appalled, but relieved that he'd never harmed their little girl.

Yes, all in all, the day had been quite an ordeal. To get away from it all, they'd finally driven up to

Tobias's house on Mount Washington for more privacy, and now, lying naked in his bed, they were staring out at the city lights below them. A summer storm had passed, leaving a startlingly clear night in its wake. Stars and skyscrapers alike twinkled in the dark night sky, looking just like the diamonds in the chastity belt they'd rescued from obscurity.

Tobias glanced away from the flame of a candle he'd lit. Truly, everything looked perfect, romantic. Dipping his head, he claimed Carla's mouth, and when she kissed him back, the rest of his body warmed. "Hmm," he said. "You feel good."

"You, too." Rolling on top of him, she wreathed her arms around his neck. The eyes that found his were warm and willing, just as relaxed as her inviting smile. It was hard to believe that just ten hours ago she'd been racing down Fifth Avenue while a maniac with a gun was chasing her. Just looking at her, Tobias felt his heart swell with admiration and love. "Are you okay?" he whispered.

She didn't answer immediately, but closed her mouth over his, using her lips to part his for a kiss. "Never better," she assured him.

He believed her, too. Her body felt as loose as a ribbon. Earlier, they'd made love, and now she was sated, satisfied. So was he. Her mind and body were free now. And while he hadn't been the one to unlock her nightmares, the way he'd always dreamed, Tobias was glad they were gone.

"Make love to me again," she murmured, shifting to her side, so he could enter her.

"Now?"

"You feel ready."

He was, despite the fact that he'd been inside her only moments before. "But you look tired."

"We'll sleep in a minute."

Pure joy coursed through him as he scooted forward, doing as she asked, thrusting inside her, gasping as she closed around him, her slick heat as dark as the night surrounding them. It was sleepy, dreamy lovemaking, and they held each other near, wrapping their arms tightly around each other in a seamless embrace, shuddering together with the sheets tucked up around their shoulders. When it was over, they moved just as seamlessly back into a deep, leisurely kiss.

"Pleasant dreams, my love," Tobias whispered then, sweeping a kiss across her forehead.

"I won't dream at all," she promised on a yawn. "Not even a fantasy. Reality is all I need."

"One more thing before you go to sleep," he murmured, dipping his head down for yet another touch of their lips.

She snuggled against his chest. "Hmm?"

"Do you think you could marry me now, Carla?"

When she glanced up, he could tell the words she'd heard that long-ago night were playing in her mind again. *If you marry, you will die.* How senseless it all had been. How unfair that a second of their pleasure should have been stolen away from them by a horrible, misunderstood warning.

But that seemed to have happened a century ago, just as long ago as when the chastity belt first found its way to America, and she said, "Of course I can marry you."

And then, as a satisfied smile stretched his lips, Tobias asked his only remaining question. "When?"

Epilogue

JUNE FIRST WAS the answer.

It was the same wedding, more or less. Same flowers, same band. Same ushers, same bridesmaids. Carla even had her original dress altered. After all, it was the gown she'd always dreamed of wearing when she married Tobias.

"Are you going to do it this time, Carla?" her father whispered.

"Yes."

That was the only hint of his tension as he led her down the aisle to give her away. Everyone here—all familiar faces—were waiting on pins and needles, ready to heave a sigh of relief, since they half expected her to run.

One of her hands curled more tightly over the sleeve of her father's tux as they went slowly down the white runner, their steps moving in time with the same music that Laura Free had suggested years ago. Hazarding a glance around, Carla smiled at some of the guests, her fingers tightening on the bouquet of cascading pink roses.

And then she took a deep breath. So much had happened in the year since Vince Gato had gone to jail; they'd waited that long to marry, since Carla had wanted to have the ceremony on the exact same day they'd originally planned. In the interim, the story had made such a splash in the *Pittsburgh Post Gazette* that Sloane Junior had backed Tobias's new clinic financially, dedicating a pristine, modern space to the university. Tobias could probably use it until he retired. Which, of course, was years away, Carla thought happily. With lots of hot, wild sex and babies in between.

Babies...which meant they'd shopped for a larger house in the suburbs. Jenna and her husband had moved upstairs, above the café. And at the other end of the block, a strange pallor had fallen over the import business, since Vince's sons had convinced him to sell while he did jail time for possessing stolen property and withholding evidence in a capital case. Probably, Vince would be paroled—since he hadn't stolen the belt himself, and since the murder he'd covered up was a century old and one for which there was still no physical evidence. Still, given his disgrace, he wasn't expected to ever return to live on Liberty Avenue.

In place of the import business, a new video store had now opened. Café business was picking up, too, since Carla's parents had approved so many changes, including the patio, which Carmine had finished building in September.

He'd also, thankfully, boarded up the secret passageway.

Not that Carla's personal experience had been for naught. Since her dreams had turned out to be memories, Tobias had wound up with more convincing data to support his dream research, and more grants had come pouring in.

"Ready?" her father whispered.

She was almost to Tobias's side. Five steps from him and the altar…then four…then two…

Everybody in the congregation was holding their breath.

She wasn't going to run, though. Not this time.

Her heart swelled as she took a final look around. Yes, she thought. Same church, same friends. But as her fingers slipped away from her father's arm, she knew it was different this time. She was different.

Same Tobias, though, she thought with a sudden smile. She should have guessed that when her father took her hand and placed it into Tobias's that her husband-to-be would murmur a soft speech. He was promising Larry that he'd care for her, protect, cherish and love her.

Without turning around, she knew that her mother and Laura Free were starting to cry. So was she. Beneath a nearly transparent veil that just grazed her chin, Carla gazed tearfully at Tobias as he wrapped his hand over her arm, and her heart lurched as her father stepped away. It was crazy, of course, but for the briefest moment, she felt as if she'd never see her dad again. And yet she would, of course. Already, she and Tobias had gone to Florida. And when the grandkids came, she and Tobias would be beating off the relatives with sticks….

"Dearly beloved…" began the priest.

The ceremony was solemn, quiet. The church hushed. By the time the priest said, "You may kiss the bride," Carla felt like a truly changed woman. She was very definitely ready for a long night in the sack with her husband. Smiling, she gazed at Tobias as he lifted the veil.

He smiled back.

His hands circled her waist, and suddenly his eyes widened. As his lips parted in surprise, hers twitched, since she was fighting not to giggle. Yep...he'd definitely found her little surprise. The solemnity of the church, by contrast to what Tobias had just discovered, was simply too much to bear.

The eyes of her luscious husband were sparkling with mischief as he took another step forward. Instead of kissing her immediately, he dipped his head and whispered, "Is that what I think it is?"

She shot him an impish grin. Searching the internet, she'd discovered that they didn't exactly quit making chastity belts in the past. Relics or not, they remained available today. "Just because I'm your wife now," she whispered wickedly, "doesn't mean I'm going to be easy."

He looked pleased. Astonished. Excited. And thoroughly in love with her teasing spirit. Not to mention as hormonal as a teenager. "Where's the key?"

She merely shrugged. "I sure do hope you remember how to pick a lock."

Captivated, he grinned. Clearly, from the hot lights gleaming in his eyes, he was wondering how he'd manage to get through all the cake-eating and rice-throwing and dancing with the relatives.

"You'd better kiss me," she mouthed, rolling her eyes toward the wedding guests he seemed to have forgotten. "The natives are restless."

"I guess I'd better," he mouthed back.

Leaning, he closed his lips tightly over hers, his hand gliding over the belt circling her waist as he sealed their marriage with a kiss that promised things really were different this time around.

Yeah, this time, he and Carla were going to have one helluva wedding night.